the CREATURE KEEPER

DAMARIS YOUNG

SCHOLASTIC

For J.B, my favourite creature

Published in the UK by Scholastic Children's Books, 2020
Euston House, 24 Eversholt Street, London, NW1 1DB, UK A division of
Scholastic Limited.

London – New York – Toronto – Sydney – Auckland
Mexico City – New Delhi – Hong Kong

Text © Damaris Young, 2020

The right of Damaris Young to be identified as the author of this work
has been asserted by her under the Copyright, Designs and Patents Act
1988.

ISBN 978 1407 19505 6

A CIP catalogue record for this book is available from the British Library

Printed by CPI Group (UK) Ltd, Croydon, CR0 4YY
Papers used by Scholastic Children's Books are made
from wood grown in sustainable forests.

1 3 5 7 9 10 8 6 4 2

www.scholastic.co.uk

Chapter 1
The Letter

The letter arrived soon after the noises began. They were tied together, one and the same.

"Read it out loud." I jiggled in my chair. "I want to know what it says!"

Pa read it slowly, his eyes flicking across the page.

Dear Mr Erwood,

I am writing to you with an offer of potential employment.

I am currently seeking an apprentice to take over the role of caring for my menagerie at Direspire Hall.

But be warned, the role is not suitable for just anyone. It requires skill, courage and ingenuity. My collection houses extraordinary creatures, who are intelligent and highly dangerous if not treated with the very best care.

As creature keeper you would be required to live permanently at Direspire Hall and would have to give up contact with anyone outside of Direspire Hall, for the safety and well-being of my creatures.

In exchange for your work, I offer a generous wage.

I look forward to meeting you.

Lady Cavendish of Direspire Hall.

Pa put the letter down on the table.

The room was silent for a moment, while we all absorbed the words.

"A generous wage," Pa muttered.

"Highly dangerous," Ma whispered.

"*Extraordinary creatures*," I breathed. The thought sent a shiver of excitement through me.

"What are extraordinary creatures like, Ma?" I asked. The sorts of animals we had around here were more of the cow and sheep variety. Although they were great in their own way, I didn't think that was what the letter was referring to.

A frown creased Ma's forehead as she poured another cup of tea. "They are *impractical*," she said. "Now a dairy cow, that's a functional creature. You feed it and it gives you milk and meat."

Milk and meat. I hated it when Ma and Pa referred

2

to our cows like that. They were more than that to me. They were family.

I ploughed on. "When was the last time you saw the extraordinary creatures, Ma?"

Ma blew on her tea to cool it down. "I was only a young girl. Back then the Direspire Hall menagerie was open for everyone to see. Terrifying beasts, they were. But then the accident happened, and after that, the gates of Direspire Hall were shut and never opened again. Thank goodness!" A haunted look passed over her face. "I knew she was keeping creatures again, I just knew it. When did we first hear the noises, Arfan? A week ago, or the week before? I thought the world was coming to an end."

"It was the week before." Pa slid the letter back into its envelope. "The cows tried to break free through the fence. That would have been the last thing we needed, if they'd got out."

"I heard the noises last night," I said. "It sounded like..." I couldn't think of a good way to describe it, so instead I took a deep breath and *roared*, which sent Crabbit the cat skittering out of the open kitchen door.

Ma gave me a cross look. "Really, Cora. It's too early for animal noises from you."

I clamped my mouth shut. Sometimes words don't really express what you want to say, so you have to roar.

"I thought she'd given up keeping dangerous creatures," Pa growled. "Something's got to be done about it."

Ma and Pa never usually liked to talk about Direspire Hall, waving off any questions I had with "that's all in the past" or "no need to bring up that unpleasantness". But I'd always been curious about the mansion on the moors.

Direspire Hall had loomed large on the moors for as long as I could remember. I had felt its presence every day growing up, as if it had its own magnetic force that was pulling me towards it.

Now the letter had confirmed the creatures were back.

And Lady Cavendish was looking for a creature keeper.

"What are you going to do about the job offer, Pa?" I asked.

Pa folded the letter and put the still-warm teapot firmly on top of it. "You wouldn't catch me taking on any creature-keeping role, not for the life of me. We've got enough on our plates, dealing with the farm and our own cattle."

Bella. That reminded me. Bella, our old dairy cow, had caught foot rot from the boggy fields and needed extra care at the moment. She was the oldest cow we had on the farm, and I'd grown up with her. I loved her with my whole heart.

I grabbed a slice of toast and jumped up. "I'm going to see Bella," I told Ma and Pa.

"Cora, wait. Sit down." Ma patted a chair. "We need to talk to you about Bella. It's important you listen carefully."

My heart paused and I felt dizzy. I sat down again slowly. "What's happened?"

"Bella's old and she's not well. We just don't have enough food for her; we have to think of the rest of the herd. And ourselves." Pa reached across the table but I jammed my hands under my armpits.

"We can't keep her. I'm sorry, Cora."

Pa's words were a horse-kick to my stomach. Before I could stop them, my words got jumbled up and stuck in my throat like thistle heads. *Not now!*

"I'm sorry, Cora. I really am," Pa said gently.

I shoved myself away from the table.

"Don't start banging and crashing around, Cora." Ma put her hand on the chipped teapot. "You know we can't afford to keep feeding Bella; we have hardly enough to feed ourselves." She tightened her shawl against the early morning draughts that stole their way into the kitchen despite Pa and me bunging up cracks in the crumbling walls with mud. "When you find your own path into farming, you'll understand."

I jumped up and ran out of the house, slamming the door behind me.

Outside, the mist smoothed out the edges of the barn, so that it appeared to float. From inside, I could hear lowing. Bella was waiting for me.

I opened the door and *mooed* in greeting.

Inside, the cow stalls were mostly empty, their occupants having been milked by Pa and let out to pasture before dawn, all except one.

I filled a clean bowl with water and added soap. Unlatching the gate, I let myself into the stall. "Hi, Bella."

The old cow turned her head towards me, but she didn't get up.

Bella was disagreeable and bullish. She swung her head at strangers and bellowed at anyone who dared get in her way. She would stamp at Pa and Ma and Crabbit until they moved out of the way or let her be. But she would let me near her. I could talk to her without my words tripping on their way out of my mouth. Just seeing her made me feel calmer. I couldn't imagine being without her.

"It's only me," I soothed. "You must be lonely, all by yourself."

Bella watched me with her brown eyes, as if to say, "What took you so long?" The fact she was still lying down worried me.

Very gently, I unpeeled the bandages.

Pa thought cows were for milking or meat, and a sick cow wasn't worth the milk. I wished he understood that they could be family as well.

Bella understood. She talked to me in her own way, and it was easier being ignored in school when I had her to talk to at home. She was like a big sister. Better than a sister, probably. She didn't quarrel with me or pinch my books, which is what sisters were known to do. I'm sure I wouldn't like that very much, although having someone to share my books with would be nice. And quarrelling wouldn't be all bad. There must be lots of times that sisters agree and team up against their ma and pa.

Maybe a sister would have helped convince Ma and Pa to keep Bella, even though she was sick, talking sense to them when anger stole my voice.

"You're going to have to try a little harder to get better, Bella." I told her, with only a small wobble in my voice. I didn't want to frighten her. "Aren't you bored of staying inside? Don't you want to play in the field with your herd?"

Belle gave an exasperated cough. With an effort, she tried to heave herself up, before collapsing back on to the straw with a groan.

"That was a good try," I said. "We can try again later, OK? Rest now."

Her hoof was swollen and sore. I pressed the soapy cloth to it.

"This might sting a little," I told her, "but it's for your own good."

Bella flinched when the water dribbled over the swelling, but she watched me with her trusting eyes as I washed her foot with soap and wrapped it up again with a clean bandage.

"I'll take care of you," I promised her.

I curled up in the straw next to Bella and pressed my face against her warm neck. She rested her head on my knee with a groan.

Being around Bella, I could think more clearly and untangle my thoughts from each other, in a way that I couldn't with people.

People just added to the knots in my brain, pulling and tweaking and snagging at my thoughts until my head was bunged up and I didn't know what to think about anything. Like with Ma and Pa, in the kitchen. My words got jumbled up and I couldn't find the ones I needed to tell them how I felt.

Besides, words were dangerous. They could be taken the wrong way or used against you. People relied on words too much, instead of listening.

Bella mooed, her breath sweet-smelling. I picked off the hay that was snarled in her coat.

"I'll find a way to help Ma and Pa look after you, Bella."

Bella lifted her head and gave me a rasping, wet lick.

"Stop!" I laughed and pushed her head gently away. I needed to go. I had to feed the other animals or I knew we'd be late for market.

"I'll be back later." I kissed her on her nose and tickled her ears, before slipping her head off my knee and standing up, brushing the straw from my trousers.

I could hear the chickens outside, cackling and scratching in their coop, grumbling at me to hurry up.

"I'm coming!" I clucked back, which only got them crowing even more. I unlocked the door and a flurry of feathers and snapping beaks erupted from the dark inside.

"Hello, Olive and Doodle and Queenie," I said in a sing-song voice, as each of them fluffed out their feathers and stretched their legs. I scattered their feed on the ground and they squawked, pecking hungrily. I watched the chickens for a while, before sneaking back to the coop and opening the back door, stretching my hand inside and feeling around for treasure. There were three eggs, perfectly speckled and warm.

Away from the chicken coop, there was a space where the grass grew tall and was allowed to seed. Untamed hedges and shrubs teemed with the sounds of birds. It was my favourite part of the farm, my wild place.

Living on a farm, everything was done in a certain way, and everything had its place. The cows were milked twice a day, every day. Once a week, we went to market in Hazelglen Town and sold eggs and jam. There was a path that you followed. There was never any question of what I would be doing for the *rest of my life* except milking cows and selling eggs and jam. Sometimes, in the middle of that overgrown space, I liked to pretend that there was another world, where adventure could be found and I could choose to follow any path I liked.

I sat down, folding my legs beneath me, calming my breathing until it was a whisper. All around me, the bees buzzed and insects hummed. A blackbird shrilled out its song, competing with a tiny wren's chirrup and a jackdaw's throaty call. I sat so still that nature forgot I existed and I melted into the undergrowth.

I couldn't stop thinking about the letter from Direspire Hall. I wished it had been me who the letter had been addressed to. I loved learning about all kinds of creatures, discovering new species and studying their behaviour and the ways they communicate. Whenever I could, I would spend hours on the moors, watching the goshawks hunting on silent wings, and the hares having furious boxing matches. The thought of spending my whole life caring for cows, only for them to be used for milk and meat made me feel as though I'd fallen into a hole in the ground. I felt trapped just thinking about it.

Sitting still was hard, especially when you felt as

though your insides were full of jumping beans, but it was worth it. From the trees to the tiniest insect, there was never a quiet moment, though it was different kind of noise to the world of people, where every noise had purpose and meaning that was difficult to understand and interpret. I understood the song of creatures and plants.

My quiet was rewarded by a tiny face peeking out of the long grass. Delighted, I watched as a mouse snuffled the chilly air, small black nose wriggling, its whiskers quivering.

I took my notebook out of my pocket and quickly, trying not to move more than I had to, I drew the little mouse peering through the grass, its whiskers tiny strokes of the pencil.

Then it was gone, scurrying into the undergrowth, only a shiver of grass to indicate where it had once been.

If I was an animal, I would be a mouse. A quiet creature that is often overlooked, but who could sneak off for an adventure whenever it liked. Ma once told me that a group of mice was called a *mischief*, which made me love them even more. Mischief could mean so many things – being playful and naughty, but also upsetting the normal way of things. Tugging at the thread and unravelling the order, so that something new could be knitted.

Cupping my hands around my mouth, I cawed loudly, aiming the sound towards the trees. With a familiar answering call, a shadow swooped from the gnarled apple tree. The crow landed on my arm with a heavy thump and his claws dug into my wrist. One beady eye blinked at me.

"Hello, Wildling crow," I whispered. "I've brought you some breakfast." I cupped my hand and filled it with birdseed that I always kept in my pocket.

I'd rescued Wildling crow from Crabbit's jaws a few summers ago, and he repaid me by visiting every now and then.

Wildling crow pecked at the seed in my hand, while I admired his glossy feathers and strong beak. Too soon, he took off again, his wingbeats clapping loudly.

Crabbit appeared from the long grass, his clever green eyes taking everything in. He was the king of the farmyard, stalking his kingdom with a snapping tail. He meowed and headbutted my arm.

"Stay away from the Wildling crow, Crabbit!" I

warned. "He's big enough to carry you away if he wanted to."

Suddenly, Crabbit ducked low to the ground, his ears flat against his head.

"What's wrong?" I said in alarm.

A strange silence fell on the meadow, the birds stopped singing. Nothing moved.

Then, out of that silence came a noise, a shrill whistle that set my teeth on edge.

I looked up at the sky and caught a glimmer. A ripple in the air, like the shimmer on soapsuds. Was it – Yes, it was!

The outline of a strange creature, flying over the meadow.

A shape with a long tail and bat-like wings.

And then it was gone, disappearing as quickly as a bubble-pop.

The birdsong returned and Crabbit skittered away towards the cottage, faster than I'd ever seen him run.

What was that creature? It had flown through the air like a swan, and was as large as one too. But it had been practically invisible, and now I was beginning to wonder if I'd imagined it. I decided to keep the strange sighting to myself, at least for now. There was no point in adding to Ma and Pa's worries.

The sun seeped through my threadbare shirt and warmed my skin. Ma and Pa would be waiting for me. I didn't want to go back inside, where I knew they would be talking in hushed voices about all the things that troubled them. The failing crops. Our crumbling home. Our empty cupboards. And me. Their strange, lonely daughter who preferred talking to animals than people. I wished that they could see that just because I was quiet didn't mean I didn't have anything to say.

Chapter 2
Market Day

The market smelled of pig fat; I could hear it sizzling from the stall that served crispy pork crackling to the hungry farmers and their families. Newly baked bread smell nipped my nose and my stomach. I tugged on Ma's sleeve. "Can I buy some bread?"

After a moment's hesitation, Ma handed me a coin. "Get a ginger cake as well, we'll have it for tea."

I ducked in front of a cart filled with pumpkins, narrowly missing getting run over, before stumbling into a flock of geese, earning myself a volley of wing blows against my legs. The herding dog barged me out of the way, skilfully taking back control of the birds.

"Watch where you're going!" The farmer gave

me a stern look. She whistled at the dog and swept past me. I recognized the strong whiff of compost and straw from the poultry farm.

The baker's shop had a queue out of the door. I ducked around the back, down an alley between the cob houses, careful to avoid the mud puddles.

I knocked on the wooden door to the baker's house, which was promptly flung open. A waft of cinnamon and butter swirled up my nose.

"What do you want?" Etta, the baker's daughter, said in greeting, a smattering of flour on her freckled face. She crossed her arms against her apron.

I managed to say, "I want to buy a loaf," before the words got stuck. I would have to leave the ginger cake for another day.

I passed over the coin Ma had given me.

Sometimes I played with Etta at school; she let me join in with her skipping rope games with her sisters. Other times she looked the other way when I waved at her.

When my words got stuck, I tried to imagine people as animals or birds, which made it easier to talk. Sometimes it worked and sometimes it didn't.

Etta reminded me of a horse that had lived in

the field next to our cows, which was friendly one moment but would try to bite your hand the next.

Etta returned with a loaf of bread. I tucked it into my cotton bag.

"Have you heard the news?" Etta dropped the coin into her pocket. "Bill lost his sheepdog, Maisie, out on the moors. He's been looking for her for days."

Bill was the shepherd who lived on the moors, just outside the town.

My heart plummeted. *Poor Maisie!* Pa didn't want us to have a dog, he said it would get in the way and be another mouth to feed, so I would visit Bill's and say hello to Maisie whenever I could. She was the sweetest creature; her tail wouldn't stop wagging whenever she was in the company of her favourite people. She loved Bill and he loved her like I loved Bella. He was her family. He would be devastated to have lost her.

"Bill said a loud noise scared her, while he was herding sheep near Direspire Hall, and she bolted." Etta's eyes widened. "He said it sounded like the Direspire monsters were back!"

I felt a shiver across my shoulders. "I've heard the noises, they sound like..." I tried to figure out how to describe the noises in words, but Etta wasn't listening.

"Bill said it was a roar that shook the ground and scattered the sheep every which way!" Etta rubbed her nose. "I always thought the place was empty. It looks like it's about to crumble into the moors."

I wondered whether Etta's ma or pa had been sent a letter from Direspire Hall. Although, with them being bakers and not farmers, I guessed they weren't the obvious choice for looking after creatures.

Etta seemed to read my mind.

"I heard that some of the farmers are getting letters, about taking up a job in Direspire Hall, but no one has taken up the job, not that I've heard of."

"Pa says nothing good can come of it. Last time there were creatures up there someone got hurt. 'Something's got to be done. Before it's too late.' She parroted her pa's voice.

I heard Etta's name being called from inside the shop. She shook her head in annoyance, sending out a cloud of flour dust.

"Bye, Cora," she said.

I nodded goodbye and went to find Ma.

The crowd had multiplied by the time I snuck

out of the alleyway. There was a storm-crackle of conversations in the air. Words like "monsters" and "letter" were on the tip of everyone's tongue, as well as darker whispers. I heard "curse" mentioned more than once, and I wondered if it was all connected to the last time that Direspire Hall was open to the public. I resolved to ask Ma and Pa about it again later. If Etta knew about it, why shouldn't I?

Looking for Ma, I ended up bumping into the person I wanted to see least of all.

Tilly.

She was leading five of her friends through the crowd, sniffing out trouble.

If Tilly was an animal, she would be a wolf, without the good bits. She was a leader who liked to prey on weaker creatures with a pinch of sharp fingers or a cruel comment. Everyone thinks Tilly is the toughest kid at school, but I knew she was scared of the rooster on her family farm. When we'd bought the chickens off Tilly's family farm, the rooster wanted to protect his hens, charging and crowing loudly, sending Tilly running back to the farmhouse. She'd been mean to me ever since.

Her group of friends always followed her, shoving and yapping at each other, barging into bystanders. In fact, my whole school felt like a pack of wolves, and I was the only sheep.

It was a relief now that the summer holidays had begun and I didn't have to go back to school until the autumn, when the growing season was over.

I had the sudden urge to melt into the pavement, to make myself as small as possible, but Tilly had spotted me, her hungry eyes sharpening.

"Beasty!" Tilly loped over. "What are you doing, hiding at the end of the alley?"

Her pack bayed with laughter.

My cheeks flushed and I felt my skin prickle, but I didn't say anything. If a dog growls at you, you don't growl back.

"Have your family got the letter yet?" Tilly grinned.

I warned myself to be careful. Tilly was setting up a trap with her words and I didn't want to fall into it. I held my tongue.

"My pa got the letter yesterday, but we've no need for the extra money," Tilly said, with a half-smile.

Tilly's family owned poultry, and they kept the chickens squashed into small barns, where they couldn't stretch their legs and wings. It was a prison, not a farm.

Tilly cocked her head to one side, as if she'd just had a thought. "But I heard your cows are old and sickly. So you probably *could* do with the money, right?"

I pushed my hands into my pockets as far as they would go. It was bad enough being taunted by Tilly, but it was worse knowing she was right. Then, with a flick of her hair, Tilly grew bored with me. "See you in school!" she sang, sweet as a kitten, and she skipped away into the crowd, her pack bouncing after her.

I found Ma near the fishmongers. I wrinkled my nose at the sharp smell of pickled herring. Ma was deep in conversation with Patty, the fishmonger. I dragged my feet, hoping to snag a thread of the discussion.

"It's not right, frightening folks. As if we haven't got enough on our plates already." Patty shucked open an oyster and sniffed it, before discarding it in a bucket.

"The whole situation just doesn't sit right with me," Ma replied. "She's got some nerve, keeping dangerous creatures in the heart of the community, then looking for someone from the town to do the dirty work! Who would want to work there, after what happened, all those years ago?"

"I remember the accident, clear as if it was yesterday," Patty said. "Even then, I remember thinking Miss Cavendish was a strange one. She couldn't have been older than thirteen, same age as I was, but she never had any friends. Surly, she was, ready with a glare but never a kind word."

Ma shook her head. "Still, that young girl. Having to bring herself up like that. We should have done more to help, after her parents..."

"It was their own fault for keeping the creatures in the first place. Accidents were bound to happen!" Patty shrugged. "Besides, Miss Cavendish, or Lady Cavendish as she is now, locked the gates. Direspire Hall is like a fortress. It was she who turned her back on the town."

Ma spotted me. "There you are, Cora." She squeezed my arm. "I thought I'd lost you to the cakes at the bakery." She thanked Patty in her soft voice and together we made our way through the crowded street.

"What happened at Direspire Hall, Ma?" I asked. "Did a creature escape?"

"I believe so, Cora. Somehow, the creature,

I think it was a large cat, rampaged through Direspire Hall, and two people got hurt, really hurt. It was a horrible thing to happen."

"What happened after that?"

"I don't know, Cora. The gates were shut that very same day. I heard Lady Cavendish got rid of all the creatures. And good riddance." I gripped hold of Ma's arm and used my body to barge through a knot of traders, so Ma could get through. Since our cottage had started letting in the cold and the wet, Ma had grown frailer, and I was extra watchful over her in crowds.

With so many farmers and fisherfolk around, it smelled like the fields and the sea had joined forces, an army of seaweed and salt and dung and mud.

The sky was painted in spring-blue and the sun prickled my skin. People were dressed in colourful shawls and shirts, shrugging off the winter like a heavy coat. Somewhere in the crowd, a fiddler played a harvest day song, a lively tune that soared to the clouds and reminded me of dancing and bonfire smoke. I wondered if Lady Cavendish had ever visited the town on market day when she was a girl, or whether she had been too busy looking after her strange creatures.

Pa had set up his stall near the end of the town square. Since we were late this morning, it must have been the only space left. I felt a pang of guilt for staying so long in the meadow with Wildling crow.

The crowd was thinner here, halfway down the alleyway that smelled of old puddles and goose droppings. A rat skittered out of the corner of my eye, before disappearing down an open grate in the road.

"No one will want to buy jam with that smell!" Ma groaned.

Pa was deep in conversation with an old man, who I recognized as Bill, the sheep farmer. His hat was pulled down over his white hair and he wore two jumpers, even in the heat. He was the town gossip, and usually spent market day going from one stall to the next, fishing for new stories, with Maisie at his side, a busy, cheerful presence; but today he seemed like a shadow of his usual self.

"Good morning, Cora." Bill gave me a sad smile. "There's no Maisie for you to say hello to today, I'm afraid."

I knew then that if Maisie was going to be found, someone had to go out and look for her. Someone who knew the moors, like me. I just had to wait for the right time to ask Pa. I couldn't bear for Bill to look so unhappy and for Maisie to be out there alone.

Ma opened up the baskets full to the brim with jam jars and began to unload them on to the table. I helped her, while Pa and Bill carried on talking.

"I turned around and she'd disappeared," Bill said to Pa, shaking his head. "The noise had scared her away. It was like the devil himself had roared. It scared the wits out of me."

"What noise?" I looked up. "What did it sound like?"

"A terrible sound, out on the moors!" Bill's eyes widened. "A groaning, like the earth was waking up beneath my feet. Maisie took off and I didn't see her again."

"I'm sorry to hear about poor Maisie," Ma said to Bill. "I hope she comes home soon." She handed Bill a jam jar. "Here. You could do with some cheering up and jam always helps."

Bill pocketed the jam, thanking her with a sad smile.

"I'm lost without Maisie. The sheep are scattered across the moors. I didn't dare search for her too close to Direspire Hall, I'm too old to be dealing with whatever monstrous creature might climb over the walls in search of a good meal."

"Maisie has most likely got herself tangled up in some briars," Pa said to him. "She'll work herself loose and be home before you know it."

"It's that wretched Direspire! That place should be torn down. Who knows what dangerous creatures she's keeping there now? And what if they escape again?" Bill shook his head. "It shouldn't be allowed. Families and livestock are at risk. In fact, this morning some of my sheep have already gone missing. Once I've bought the weekly shop, I'll head back out and continue looking."

"We can organize a search party if she's not back by tomorrow." Pa brushed his beard with his hand. "I'll talk to some of the other farmers and see if they can spare a few of their scent-dogs."

"I could go and look for Maisie!" I said. "Please, Pa, let me try. I could go after market, before it gets dark—"

"You won't go on those moors, Cora. Do you hear?" Pa growled. When he spoke like that there was no arguing with him.

"That Direspire Hall. It's not right." Bill shook his head again. "If I had my way, the place would be searched and whatever *abominations* are being hoarded would be dealt with. For the good of the whole town."

Dealt with? I didn't like the sound of that.

"Something will be done about it soon enough, mark my words," Pa said. "Things can't carry on the way they are."

Bill and Pa exchanged a grim look. Then Bill tapped his cap with his finger in a salute and said his goodbyes, walking back the way he came, through the thinning crowd.

My heart ached for him. I knew how much he loved Maisie, how worried about her he would be. I was worried too. It wasn't like Maisie not to come home; she knew those moors as well as Bill did. Something must have scared her badly. And it sounded like that something had come from Direspire Hall.

Although it was quieter down the alley, there was still enough footfall to sell some of the vegetables and jam. With each purchase I felt a tiny weight leave my shoulders.

Morsels of conversation dropped from passers-by.

"I took one look at the letter and tore it up, put

it straight on the fire. Who does she think she is?" a woman tutted. "Asking people to put their lives at risk."

"It's shameful. You would have thought she would show a little more respect." Her friend shook her head.

I rearranged the jam on the table, making sure all the labels faced outwards. The thought of Maisie lost all alone nagged at me like a splinter under the skin. Like Maisie and Bill, I knew the moors better than most people. I would spend all day watching the roe deer, and waiting for a mole to surface, hunting for new territory. I knew I could find her, if Ma and Pa would let me go. And if that meant getting closer to Direspire Hall, maybe even seeing what was inside – well, that couldn't be helped, could it?

I was only aware of how quiet the alleyway had become when Ma grabbed hold of my shoulder, pinching it tight. She pulled me closer.

A man walked towards us, with his arm in a sling, a bandage wrapped tightly around his upper arm, dark spots soaking through the fabric. He caught me staring and his mouth clamped into a taut line. He scurried past.

"Is he all right?" Ma hissed at Pa. "Should we see if he needs anything? Maybe some jam?"

I hid a grin behind my hand. Ma thought jam could cure *everything*. Aching bones, sadness and sore stomachs could all be solved with a spoonful of jam.

But the man had already disappeared, slipping through the crowd that parted for him like wind through a cornfield. A moment passed, then the buzz of conversation started up.

"Who was that man?" I prised Ma's fingers off my shoulder.

"That's Mr Johnson," Ma replied. "He works at Direspire Hall, but I've never seen him at the market before. He usually buys supplies for Lady Cavendish directly from the baker and the larger farmers." Ma tapped her fingers on the table, like she did when she was concerned. "Poor man, he looks awfully battered. Who knows what he has to deal with behind the walls of Direspire Hall, with those wretched creatures?"

Pa fixed his gaze in the direction the man had gone. "There's no amount of money in the world that would get me to work at that cursed place," he said.

*

Pa helped Ma up into the cart. She nestled up against the empty potato sacks and tucked her shawl around herself. She looked like a doll, her hair neat and her cheeks blossoming with the heat of the day's sunshine. "It's been a long day," she yawned, closing her eyes.

We followed the trail back to our hilltop farm, as the sun melted in the horizon, a candle reaching the end of its life. With the oncoming night, my thoughts were drawn back to Maisie. I let the seed of a plan begin to grow in my mind.

We reached the edge of the moor, where the grazing land turned to gorse and prickly heather. The clip-clop of Merlin's hooves softened on the grass and I could hear the churring call of a grouse. If Maisie had been frightened, she would have sought out somewhere she felt safe. Somewhere hidden. I'd spent so much time on the moors, searching for the secret spaces to study creatures, that I knew of lots of places where a lost dog might find herself stuck. Badger burrows and fox dens and gorse hideaways where sheep shelter from the wind.

I was engrossed in considering all the places Maisie might be stuck, when we turned up the path towards home. Turning to face our cottage, I saw that something was wrong with its shape. It looked lopsided, as if it had lost its balance and couldn't get back up.

Pa cursed under his breath.

"What's going on?" said Ma sleepily. She sat up, patting her hair.

"The roof," I said, a heavy weight on my chest. "The roof has collapsed."

Chapter 3
Lost Dogs Want to be Found

"Keep out of the way, Cora, while we inspect the damage. The last thing we need is for you to get hurt." Pa sighed. "I'll call when it's safe to come indoors."

I was always needed "out of the way". I was never in the right place at the right time. I wanted to *help*. But Pa had already turned his back and was conferring with Ma in low tones as they stared up at the sunken roof.

I decided to see how Bella was doing. I led Merlin to his field, before filling his feed bucket up. From there, I could see the moors stretching as far as the horizon, endless heather and bracken. A fog had started to roll in from the sea, as the night took over.

On a clear day, I could see Direspire Hall, looming on the moors like a dark cloud, but the fog hid it from view tonight. That didn't stop me squinting into the growing darkness and imagining an escaped creature, roaming loose on the moor. I shivered, half with fright and half with delight. I wondered whether I had imagined the strange bird in the meadow earlier, with its translucent bat-like wings and haunting whistling call. Tomorrow morning, I would keep an eye out for it again.

Leaving Merlin to his supper, I ran to the barn and swung the door open.

"Mooo!" I lowed and five heads turned to face me.

Petal, Pebble, Seashell, Bumblebee ... and Bella!

I ran to the last stall. "You're up!" I shouted.

Bella snorted, her impatience confirming her wellness.

Taking the rungs two at a time, I jumped over her gate.

Bella was putting weight on her feet, all of them.

Gently, I ran my hand down her leg, the one that had been so swollen and sore. It felt cool to the touch now, and Bella didn't flinch. I felt a swell of hope that even the worry of the fallen-in roof couldn't dampen. Did this mean that things might just be all right?

I heard Pa calling for me, his faint voice heavy with tiredness.

Back inside the cottage, I found that Ma and Pa had made a bed up in the living room for me, a mug of soup on the table for supper.

"This is only temporary, Pumpkin." Pa plumped my pillows and tucked the bedsheet around the mattress on the floor. "Things will be back to normal soon."

Ma and Pa said goodnight, taking their mugs of soup with them.

Lying down on the mattress, I cuddled Crabbit close. He purred against my chest. I was relieved he hadn't been inside when the roof had fallen in.

It was strange, sleeping in the living room. I could hear the drip-drip-drip of the tap in the kitchen and the groan of the wind down the chimney.

It was dusty too. The thatched roof had fallen in over the back of the house, where my room had been. Dust specks swirled in the stream of moonlight through the window, like snowflakes. The thought of having a house with a broken roof when it *did* snow in winter, was troubling. Could we fix it before then? I knew we needed everything we made at the market just to keep the animals fed and well, and while I was delighted that Bella had recovered, I was sure Pa would think only of the extra mouth to feed. Where on earth were we going to find the money to repair the roof? I turned it all over in my mind before I remembered.

The letter.

Generous wage, it had said.

Pa had said he wouldn't go, but what if I applied? What if I could be the creature keeper of Direspire Hall? No. I was being silly. Why would the lady of Direspire Hall employ a child to look after her creatures?

Crabbit hissed. He leaped out of my arms and scooted under the dresser.

"What is it, Crabbit?" I sat up, throwing the bedcovers off.

Outside, the wind picked up and rattled the window panes. The draught brought with it another sound, an animal howling.

"It's all right," I whispered. "It's coming from Direspire Hall, too far away to be any danger to you."

But Crabbit wasn't coming out from under the

dresser.

I thought of Maisie again, out on the moors, listening to the same howl in the wind.

She would be so frightened.

I slipped out from the warm nest of blankets and shivered as my feet touched the cold stone floor. Quick and quiet, I got dressed and eased up the window, until the curtains formed ghosts in the chill breeze.

From here, I could see the misty edges of the moor.

Maybe I could look for Maisie now? Ma and Pa didn't have to know, not if I was back before dawn.

As I walked past the kitchen table, I saw that the letter was where Pa had left it, under the teapot on the kitchen table. I tucked it into my pocket, my heart hammering. I felt horribly guilty. It was addressed to Pa, not me. I was only borrowing it, I told myself. I wasn't even sure why I was taking it. It was the middle of the night; it wasn't as if I could just knock on the door and ask for a job at two o'clock in the morning. Besides, finding Maisie was more important than all of that.

I packed a torch, a portable lamp, my pocket knife and my notebook into my backpack and grabbed a jar of jam from the table and tucked it into the bag too. *You never know when you might need jam*, Ma always told me and she was usually right.

I clambered out on to the window sill. It wasn't much of a jump – our cottage was built low on the ground to protect it from storms – but still, I didn't want to crush the flower bed outside the window, for fear of giving away clues of my night-time adventure. I landed with a thump on the grass. Heart beating, I waited for a light to turn on, but the house stayed in darkness.

I crept across the moonlit garden and eased the garden gate open, wincing at its squeak of protest at being woken up at this late hour. Luckily, the creak from the metal hinge joined in with the croaks from the speckle-frogs in the pond near the barn.

Once I'd reached the dirt road, I knew I was safe from being seen from the house. My pulse quickened, every smell sharper than in the day. Even the flowers smelled different, as if to attract otherworldly insects that only appeared at night.

If I was caught, I'd be in trouble. Ma and Pa didn't like me going to the moors on my own at the best of times, and after what Pa had said earlier I knew he'd be doubly angry. But Maisie was in trouble and I knew I had to find her, then deal with the consequences. If a creature was in trouble, I had to help, otherwise it would eat me up inside.

If Merlin was surprised to see me at this hour of the night, he didn't show it. He came over to the gate and nuzzled my shoulder.

"Do you want to help me find Maisie?" I unbolted the gate and heaved it to one side.

Merlin trotted out, lifting his feet up high. In the moonlight, his grey hair was almost silver and he tossed his head as if he was a young horse again.

I slipped the bridle on, not bothering with the saddle and stirrups. I stepped up on the bars of the metal gate and sprang on to Merlin's broad back. He skittered, then settled down.

"Let's go!" I whispered in his twitching ear and patted him on the neck.

For an old horse, he seemed to come alive in the night, cantering sure-footed along the path that led to the moors, the cornfields rushing past in silver and gold.

I gripped on with my legs and held tight to his mane, only needing to direct him with a lean to the left or right. I'd been riding Merlin ever since I was able to walk and we could very nearly read each other's thoughts.

Before long, the fields turned to open spaces and the road dissolved into sheep trails. The ground grew springy as Merlin's hooves tramped the bracken and moss. I breathed in the sleepy smell of heather, and the sharp night smells of hare and fox. From the sea, the fog rolled in, hiding the path underfoot, slowing our pace.

We walked until the shape of Direspire Hall jutted out of the surrounding moorland, its black edges jagged against the fog. It was as out of place as a buzzard nesting among sparrows. The salt-smell of the sea blew towards us from the cliff edge. In my throat, fear caught like a burr.

Using the walls of Direspire Hall as a marker, I found my bearing. I knew there were badger burrows to the south side of Direspire, large enough for a dog to bolt into if she was scared enough.

I kept the grey walls on my left. I'd never seen the lights on in the windows of the manor house, no twitched curtain or silhouette against the glass panes. It looked abandoned, with ivy clinging to the walls like cobwebs. I imagined the dead, empty windows alive with eyes, watching me approach in the dark. I thought of the letter in my pocket, feeling silly now. I would never be brave enough to knock on the door and ask for a job.

As we moved closer, Merlin twitched his ears back and forth, listening to sounds too far away or too low for my ears. He snorted, tossing his head and pulling on the reins.

The towers and turrets of Direspire Hall jutted towards the night sky. Each part of the great building seemed to twist and turn in different directions at every opportunity. The tallest turret scraped the low cloud that always hung over the hall. I didn't think I'd ever seen clear skies over Direspire Hall, not even in summer. There was always a scrap of grey that clung to the turret like a ragged cloth caught on barbed wire.

Surrounding Direspire Hall were imposing walls. They were a snarl of bared teeth that bit into the soft moorland. Despite the tingling fear in my blood, I longed to peek over the walls to see what creatures might be there...

On the other side of Direspire lay the sea.

The sea, the one that bordered our part of the world, wasn't like any other. It had a mind of its own. Ma said it had eyes and ears and even teeth, and that it would gobble you up if you weren't careful.

But to me, the sea and the moors were *free*. With the farm behind me, I felt lighter, light enough that the wind could pick me up and carry me away, and I half-wished it would. I might end up where no other human had been, where adventure was.

I was so engrossed in my thoughts that I almost lost my balance when Merlin stopped suddenly.

He nervously trotted to either side, as if unsure of his next step.

"All right, I'll walk with you from here." I slipped off his back, landing in the soft moss. "Let's see what we can find."

I wasn't afraid of the dark, or the moorland, but my heart pounded in my chest as the wind whipped my hair and tugged at my clothes, like impish ghosts. Overhead, clouds gathered, snuffing out the stars one by one. It smelled like rain was on the way. I had to hurry.

I was alert to every sound, scanning the expanse of heather and bracken for a flash of white that would mean Maisie was nearby.

I knew this was close to where I had once found a large abandoned badger burrow last summer, while picking bilberries with Ma. If Bill had kept away from Direspire Hall, he wouldn't have stumbled upon it. Maisie might be lost inside.

"Come on, Merlin, not far now," I encouraged the old horse.

We walked a sheep trail that curved around Direspire Hall, following the grey walls at a distance. I whistled with my thumb and index finger, three sharp notes, then listened. There was an answering howl, so faint that I thought I might have imagined it. I whistled again.

This time, I was sure I'd heard it. "This way, Merlin!"

The moors are where the sheep graze among the wild creatures, becoming half wild themselves. The open space is where you'll find the prey and the hunters, the birds and the burrowers. Ice-cold air nipped my ankles, making me shiver.

Whistling again, I stopped and listened. A yelp from nearby, weak but undeniable. It was a dog. Not a fox or a badger, but a frightened dog, lost and alone.

"Maisie!" I shouted out and the yelping grew into a frenzy, urging me closer.

I spotted the dark mouth of a badger burrow.

"Maisie?" I called down. I was rewarded by a small pink nose and a howl of gratitude.

Pushing aside the brambles, I lay on my stomach and reached into the hole. A bundle of wriggly fur and slobbering tongue greeted me, making me laugh in delight.

She was caught in a tangle of briers, their thorns embedded in her thick coat.

"Hold on, Maisie." With my pocket knife in one hand, I leaned into the burrow and very carefully cut the briers. "Hold still."

With a slice of the knife, Maisie was free and I pulled her out of the hole. She squirmed into my lap, knocking us both over.

"You silly pup, you had us worried." Relief flooded through me as Maisie's warm breath melted against my cheek. She was alive and safe.

"Come on, Maisie, let's take you home."

Guiding Merlin over to a tree stump, I hauled Maisie on to his back, then climbed on myself. Maisie was a small dog and Merlin was not easily daunted, so it didn't take long until Maisie and I were settled comfortably on his back.

"Well done, Merlin!" My heart swelled with pride for the old horse.

The fortress-like walls of Direspire Hall were now on my right side, obstructing my view of the sea, even though I could still hear the waves lashing down on the rocky shoreline and smell the salt and seaweed.

Merlin was skittery now, leaping to the left, as if the path was blocked by invisible enemies. He seemed to want to keep as much distance between us and Direspire Hall as possible.

His nerves set mine alight and I tried hard to stop myself from starting at every shadow and sound. The wind began to pick up, buffeting us from every direction.

"Woah, Merlin," I soothed, through chattering teeth.

Suddenly, thunder rumbled across the sky. I felt a prickling of rain on my face. The moor was illuminated by a flash of blinding light, followed by another drumroll of thunder.

Merlin whinnied, a shriek that shattered my courage into pieces and backed away from the path. "Hold still, Merlin! Calm down. Home isn't far." I gripped hold of the reins.

I guided Merlin back on to the trail for the umpteenth time. "Keep to the path, Merlin, otherwise we'll get lost on the open moor." I tried to keep some calm in my voice.

Then, I heard what Merlin must have been listening to all along. A sound I had heard before, a groan that brought to mind a sinkhole opening up, or a cave crumbling in on itself, rattling my bones and almost frightening me off Merlin's back.

"Woah, boy!" I soothed the horse. Maisie shivered and cowered against me, pushing her face under my armpit. I clutched her to my chest.

The groan sounded again, twisting itself into a growl that made me feel hot and then cold, before stretching itself into a wail, so taut I felt I could have cut myself on the keen edge.

Merlin tossed his head and reared. With Maisie pressed to my chest, I lost my balance and slipped off his back, crashing to the ground with a thump. Maisie squirmed out of my arms and shot down the path towards Bill's cottage, Merlin close behind.

They disappeared into the darkness, leaving me clutching my sides and gasping for air.

Checking to see if I'd broken any bones, I cautiously stood up.

"Well, that's not brilliant, Cora," I scolded myself. The prickle of rain turned into a downpour, soaking through my jumper. With a lightning storm, I knew better than to go wandering out on to open moors.

Direspire Hall stood next to me. Surely it would be safe enough to shelter from the storm, as long as I was outside the grounds themselves? I didn't have much other choice. I pressed against the walls and waited for the storm to pass.

Chapter 4

Howling at the Sky

I must have fallen asleep, because it was the chirping of a skylark that woke me. Although I was still damp from the rain, the early morning sun was warm. A pebble suddenly landed on my lap. Puzzled, I picked it up.

I couldn't see where it had come from. I looked up to find that I'd taken shelter near a stone archway. Beneath the archway, heavy metal gates were closed shut. Elaborate curls and spirals of metal rusted brown, with overgrown buddleia reaching through, their purple and red flowers attracting butterflies. Through the bars, all I could make out were oak trees and a tangle of briars, with a path that curved to the right and out of sight. A redwing called out a furious warning, a harsh *yakyakyak* before the tiny bird whirled away into the dense woodland.

A boy, about my age, with a dirty face and blonde hair that stuck right up, watched me from behind the gates.

"Hello!" said the boy, and grinned through the bars, showing two rows of crooked teeth. "I've been throwing pebbles at you, trying to wake you up. You were snoring."

Who was this? Direspire Hall had been closed to the public for years. Could this boy be part of the Cavendish family?

The boy hopped from one foot to the other, as if the ground was hot coals. He reminded me of a frog, with big pale blue eyes.

"I'm Griff. I'm the gardener here," he said. That would explain the streaks of mud across his face, I guessed. I'd thought the only person working here was the man with the dour face at the market.

Griff looked no older than me, but I had never seen him in school.

He bounced from one foot to the other. "What were you doing sleeping outside in the storm? What's your name? Do you live nearby?" The questions rained down and my voice jammed in my throat. I took a step back.

Griff's eyes went wide. "Don't leave!" He looked so crestfallen that I stepped forward again.

I wanted to ask him about the creatures inside Direspire Hall. Sometimes it was easier to communicate without words. Thinking of the strange noises I heard the night before, I took a deep breath and howled at the sky.

"Ahoooooooooooooooo!"

When I had finished, I paused for breath and looked at Griff to see whether he would laugh at me like the kids at school. He was gaping at me.

"That was brilliant!" He cupped his mouth and howled, his head thrown back.

"Ahoooooooooooooooo!"

I burst out laughing. Griff was almost as good at creature noises as me.

"My name is Cora," I said, and he nodded.

"Pleased to meet you, Cora," he said.

There was something likeable about Griff. Maybe it was the surprise of finding someone my age here at Direspire Hall, after being warned to avoid the place for so long. If Griff was here, it surely couldn't be as dangerous as everyone said.

Griff kicked at the gate, making it clang. "If I had the keys, I'd let you in and show you the creatures."

"Oh, I would love that!" My arms prickled with goose pimples at the thought of seeing the Direspire creatures.

He thought for a moment. "Maybe there is a way ... Last time I checked, Lady Cavendish was in her study and Mr Johnson – he's the butler – was in the library. I could sneak you in, if you promise to be quiet and careful."

My heart leaped into my mouth. "I promise!"

Griff pointed left of the gate, further into the woods behind the wall.

"There's a tree growing against the wall that overlooks the gardens. If you can climb the tree, you can jump on to the shed roof below! It's a bit of a drop, but you should be fine."

He raced off without waiting for my answer. A tickle of trepidation started at the base of my spine and zinged all the way up my back, but I ignored it. I wasn't going to let it stop me from seeing the creatures.

The twisted tree was easy to spot. It grew in a snarl against the grey bricks of the wall, its roots cracking the foundations like nothing was going to stand in its way.

This is your chance to change your mind. You could run home and no one would be any wiser.

"Cora?" A small voice hissed over the wall. "Do you think you can climb over?"

"I think so." The tree looked frighteningly high now that I was standing right underneath it.

I tightened the straps on my backpack. The first branch was easy enough, but I couldn't keep the wobble out of my legs as I climbed higher.

"Don't look down," I heard Griff say, which meant that I looked down immediately. The ground rolled like the sea.

Digging up all the courage I could find, I pulled myself up to the height of the wall.

I glanced up at the peak of the towers, just visible through the tall trees. Direspire Hall really did look like a hawk nest, built among the trees. I felt as though I was standing on the edge of a cliff, about to step out into thin air. The air smelled like the lost parts of a forest, where leaves were left to rot and trees could grow where they pleased. With my heart in my mouth, I leaped from the tree on to the stone wall. Perched on the wall, I clung on with both hands, my legs dangling into the shadows below.

"That's it, you're almost over!" Griff grinned from the ground, looking as small as a mouse. He stood next to a wooden shed.

I hauled myself into a crouching position. "What do I do now?"

"You'll have to jump on to the shed. It's safe. I think." Griff called out, "Go on, Cora!"

I pushed off and landed heavily on my feet on top of a wooden roof.

I took a second to catch my breath. Then the enormity of the situation hit me.

I was in Direspire Hall. The place that everyone spoke about in hushed whispers. Ever since I'd been small, I'd been warned about the place, but that had only made me want to see over the walls even more. Now, those warnings nipped at me.

Swinging my legs over the shed roof, I dropped to the ground and looked around. The walls were less intimidating once you were inside, with tall trees obscuring swathes of them. There was a stillness, without the wild winds of the moors battering me from either side.

"Come on," said Griff, and he started walking.

I followed Griff up the driveway, through the cluster of ancient oak trees.

The grounds opened up and I caught my breath. A field filled with unruly rows of flowers, like tulips, roses and carnations, spilled from their beds and grew even in the cracks of the drive. Bees and butterflies swarmed in brightly coloured clouds.

It was wild and muddled and wonderful.

"I've tried to imagine what it would be like inside," I told Griff. "From outside, the place always looked abandoned."

"It does look a bit untidy, but Lady Cavendish says she can't get anyone to help with the upkeep of the place. No one wants to work at Direspire Hall, only Mr Johnson, and me and Ma." Griff ducked behind an oak tree and I followed, so that we were both hidden from view of the house. "I haven't met anyone my own age since we arrived. It's nice to be able to talk to someone who's not bossing me around."

Griff was unlike the other children at school – he was being nice to me, for one thing. Maybe that was only because he was desperate for company, being stuck behind the walls of Direspire Hall, but still – he was going to show me the creatures! I followed behind as he hopped and skipped through the long grass.

"Will you get in lots of trouble if they find out you've helped me sneak in?" I asked.

Griff nibbled on his thumbnail. "We'll be really careful not to get found out."

That meant yes, I thought.

Staying doubled over, Griff crept along behind a tall hedge and I copied him. Then I stopped, my eyes catching on something extraordinary.

"Is that a fountain?" I gasped.

In the middle of the path, there was a muddy pond with a statue of the winged horse, rearing up on its hind legs, with hooves that clipped the sky, streaked with green algae. I'd never seen anything like it.

Griff tugged me back towards the hedge.

"Yes, but it hasn't worked for years." He shook his head at me. "You're going to have to be more careful. We can't let anyone see you."

We followed the hedge as it wound around Direspire Hall.

"There's an orchard!" I exclaimed, spotting the gnarled limbs of apple trees and the white flowers of a pear tree in the distance, just like the ones we had on the farm. From a row of beehives came a low drone.

"Keep your voice down." Griff picked up his pace. I ran to catch up with him.

"The building is so much larger than it looks from outside the walls!" I said, craning my neck to look up at the highest turret. It was the grandest house I'd ever seen, yet it had a dishevelled feel to it, like a duke who'd lost his reading glasses.

As always, the clouds hung low above us. I spotted a wood nearby, where the trees were so tall that the tops of them disappeared into the clouds, their silvery leaves appearing to melt into the haze. They grew on the side of the grounds nearest the sea cliff, hidden behind the bulk of Direspire Hall, which is why I must have never noticed them before.

"I've never seen trees like those," I said, pointing to them. "They're so tall!"

Griff followed my gaze. "They're the whistling trees," he said. "I don't like going there by myself. All the trees look the same, and they whistle in the wind. It sounds like ghosts." He shivered.

Whistling trees! How wonderful.

Griff motioned for me to follow him, as he pressed his back to the walls of Direspire Hall. "Quick, Cora," he called over his shoulder.

The walls of Direspire Hall were lined with the skeletons of dead ivy. I ran my hand over them as I walked and the brittle plants crumbled, along with bits of the brickwork.

I dusted my hands off on my dungarees.

Looking around, I tried to snatch a glimpse of the creatures, imagining them hiding from sight behind the sagging shape of the dilapidated shed or scurrying through the long grass. When you're on the hunt for extraordinary creatures, everything looks strange. Branches become snaking limbs. Faces appear in the crags of the rocks and even the morning sunlight shimmers on the leaves like water on scaly skin.

Unruly hedgerows grew higgledy-piggledy, forming something that might once have been a maze, but were now so overgrown that the paths were lost. Griff didn't appear to be the most efficient gardener.

"Here we are!" Griff declared suddenly.

We turned the corner of the manor house and I found myself staring at a magnificent domed glasshouse, as big as our cow barn, that caught every sunbeam in a shattering display of glittering lights. I gasped. I had never seen anything so brilliant; it took my breath away.

"This is the glasshouse." Griff cracked open the door. "The creatures are inside!"

Chapter 5

The Glasshouse

Griff led me into the cast-iron and glass structure. It looked like it was carved from ice. I expected to shiver as we stepped into the open doorway, but inside it was hot and stuffy. Fragrant lilies grew in large pots near the entrance, giving off a heady smell that made me feel woozy. Nearby, cherry trees grew almost to the ceiling, their branches heavy with the red fruit. A path of pebbles led into the interior, heading towards the distant sound of splashing water. A cloud of mist hung over everything.

"Do the creatures live *here*?" I struggled to keep my voice low. "This is the most amazing place I've ever seen!"

It was like another world compared to the

moors and the farmland I knew. There were more strange trees, with spiky leaves and smooth, shiny trunks that stretched towards the pale morning sky filtering through the glass. There was so much colour – deep red flowers as big as my head, delicate yellow hanging plants that looked like lace curtains, and all the shades of green you could think of. I felt dizzy trying to take it all in.

And the smells! I could taste the air, with honey-sweetness and pepper on my tongue. My stomach rumbled, reminding me that it was breakfast time.

The thought of Ma and Pa waking up and finding me gone dampened the excitement. I should have left a note. But it was too late now. I'd face the music later.

"Where are the creatures?" I asked, ducking beneath a branch that drooped low with heavy purple fruit as we walked further into the enclosure.

Griff skipped from one paving stone to the next. "Follow me!"

Towering trees, their trunks tall and stalk-like, brushed the glass ceiling. Yellow ferns waved in the warm, circulating air, and vines clambered up and swung down off every available branches, trunk and stem.

"Watch out for the macaw, it's territorial!" Griff called over his shoulder.

"What's a macaw?" I shouted back, as an explosion of red, blue and yellow burst out of the vine-covered tree.

I ducked just in time to see a brightly coloured bird sail over my head and disappear among the treetops. I straightened up, staring at the place the bird with the jewelled wings had disappeared into.

"That bird is huge!" I gasped.

It's all very well knowing that there was more to the world than our tiny town, but seeing all this with my own eyes was like something else altogether. Everything in the glasshouse felt dreamlike, unreal.

"Careful of your step." Griff stepped over a brown boulder. "Or you'll tread on the tortoises."

"What are tort—" I began, then the boulder moved, all by itself, stopping me in my tracks. A grey head popped out of the boulder and glared at me disapprovingly.

"It's alive!" I called out. "This rock is alive!"

I dropped down on my hands and knees and watched as the creature strode off on four short legs and disappeared through the fronds.

"You'll find them all over the place." Griff grinned. He seemed to revel in his role as tour guide.

Around another twist in the path and we came across an enclosure, made of metalwork and glittering glass panes.

"What's inside?" Curiosity burned like a fire in my chest.

"They're the moonbirds." Griff nodded at the viewing window. "Take a look!"

I leaned forward. From behind the glass, a cloud of silver birds swarmed around the space within, wings like slices of pure moonlight. They fluttered against glass, scratching at it with sharp claws. Their tiny eyes were like glittering diamonds.

Their enclosure was littered with dead branches splattered in droppings, and the floor was covered in a white blanket of feathers. I could see their beaks opening and closing, but couldn't hear anything.

"They aren't making any sound," I said, puzzled.

"The enclosure is soundproofed," Griff said. "They'll make your ears bleed if you hear their song." Griff tapped the glass with his finger. "You have to wear special ear protection if you go inside.

You wouldn't want them to be set free."

I stepped closer and pressed my hand against the glass pane. It was ever so slightly cold and I could feel tiny reverberations, hundreds of voices hammering against the inside of the glass, trilling against my palm. I could almost hear the undulations of the song in my ear, so achingly sorrowful that tears prickled behind my eyes.

"They are beautiful," I breathed. I had spent hours watching the creatures of the moorland, from the grandest stag to the smallest dormouse, and I had never seen anything like these birds.

We made our way further along the path, leaving the moonbirds behind. The glasshouse stretched up into a peaked roof, the glass panes secured in place by elaborate cast iron brackets, with the metalwork made to look like flowers and vines. As I craned my neck to admire it, a swarm of butterflies rose into the air, some as large as birds and others only a thumb-sized smudge. Their wings shimmered, some gold and silver, some bright purple and red, the colours of the sunset.

It was hot in here, and stuffy. I wiped the sweat from my forehead with my sleeve and a butterfly with large brown wings landed on my finger. I stopped still, holding in my breath.

The butterfly slowly opened its wings, revealing what appeared to be two eyes that glared at me crossly; then the wings shimmered and the eyes changed, suddenly sorrowful. I felt a sob catch in my throat. The sorrow in the eyes on the butterfly's wings felt almost too much to bear.

The butterfly fluttered and flew off, and I snapped out of the trance.

"Butterflies that can affect your mood," explained Griff.

I watched as a dainty blue butterfly landed on a shiny green plant which had strange red petals with hairs protruding all around the sides. I leaned closer, to count the black spots on its wings, but the plant's petals snapped shut, trapping the poor butterfly inside.

"No!" I gasped, before stepping back, in case the plant decide it wanted a bigger meal.

I could hardly believe the wonders in the glasshouse. Carnivorous plants! Mood-changing butterflies! Moonbirds! What would I find next?

Griff stopped in front of a small wall. "Take a look here!"

I rushed over, almost stumbling in my eagerness.

It was another enclosure, with walls that came up to my waist. I leaned over the wall to look inside. The enclosure was made up of sand, punctuated by small hills covered in tough, brown grass. I peered around the area, hunting for any sign of what creature might live here. But as hard as I tried, there was no movement.

"What's in here?"

"A pangolin!" Griff said. "That's what Lady Cavendish calls it. I've never seen it, I think it only comes out at night. I bet it's got razor-sharp claws," he said with a shudder, taking a step back.

"A pangolin?" I was realizing just how little I knew about the creatures of the world. There was so much I hadn't seen, so much I didn't know about.

Another enclosure was revealed behind a twist in the path, almost hidden between the tall trees with frond-like leaves. This time, the enclosure was a cage, with thick metal bars protecting us from whatever was inside.

And then I saw it.

The creature in the enclosure looked like a cat who hadn't figured out how to stop growing. From its whiskers to its flat, snapping tail, its fur shimmered with blue and black stripes that merged with the shadows. Its four paws were huge and webbed and it walked forward a few steps with a strange rolling gait, as if it was unaccustomed to walking on land.

But it was its eyes that pulled me in, as bright as emeralds, drawing me closer to the bars of the enclosure. It was breathtakingly beautiful.

"Don't get too close," Griff warned. "It's a seacat. Lady Cavendish told me that it came from the ocean, where it hunts fish and turtles."

I could see the creature was formidable, but this majestic animal with its bent head didn't strike any fear into my heart. It looked like its fighting spirit had been used up long ago. The cage itself was filthy, with nothing to amuse the creature, just trampled dirt and a smell of damp and rot. Its beautiful coat of midnight blue and black was matted and dull.

The creature opened its mouth and snarled. It was loud, but it didn't sound quite the same as the rumbling, howling noises that I'd heard before, and it wasn't nearly loud enough to scatter Bill's sheep and terrify the farmers. Maybe there was another creature responsible for making those sounds.

Gazing at the seacat, my heart ached for the

creature. I suddenly felt angry at Lady Cavendish, for keeping the creatures in cages that were small and filthy. These animals were miserable. No wonder she needed a creature keeper!

I mimicked the seacat's roar, rolling my voice into a swell and then trailing off into a purr.

"Rawwhhhrrrrrrr!"

It wasn't the exact sound, but it was hopefully close enough to show the seacat that I was trying to learn its language. That I wanted to understand it. That's what everyone wants really. The seacat flicked its ear, its eyes focused on me for a moment, before padding away to the murky pond in the middle of the enclosure. It slipped beneath the layer of algae, until only its eyes, which were positioned on the top of its head, were visible. "Why hasn't the cage been cleaned?" I quizzed Griff, feeling miserable for the creature. "The poor animal is pacing around, with nothing to do with itself!"

Griff wiped his nose with his sleeve. "Lady Cavendish has been busy. She stays in her study, reading books and painting."

I peered through the bars of the cage. "That

pond needs refilling with clean water, and some trees should be planted, to provide shade. Our cows have shade in their field, where they wait out the hottest part of the day. Otherwise the seacat will get heat sick!" I sighed at the lack of common sense. "Who's looking after the creatures, if Lady Cavendish isn't?"

But Griff was distracted. His eyes flitted around uneasily, as if listening for something or someone. "We should hurry. Mr Johnson will be out of the library soon."

We clipped over a wooden bridge that spanned a large pond. Water lilies floated on the still surface and I could see my reflection when I leaned over the side, as well as the glass ceiling above me.

Tiny fish flitted under the surface, gold and silver. Then a shadow shot out from the dark part of the water and one of the silver fish disappeared, leaving only the faintest ripple. A fish the size of a house cat lurked beneath the lilies.

"Did you see that?" I shouted at Griff. "There's a huge fish eating the small fish!"

Griff peered over the handrail. "Mr Johnson threatened to throw me to the perch once, when I wasn't quick enough to mow the lawn."

"He doesn't sound like a very nice person."

Griff tugged at my sleeve, leading me over the bridge. "Let's just make sure he never finds out you were here," he said.

But I didn't want to leave! Now that I'd seen what was here, I wanted the role of creature keeper. How could I go back to the farm, when I *knew* that I was the right person for the job? I had never been this certain about anything in my life.

"Here we are!" Griff halted at another glass enclosure. This one was large, with four glass walls reaching up to the ceiling. A hissing sound seemed to come from within, from a machine puffing out steam. "This is the enclosure for the glass dragon!"

"A glass dragon?" I gasped. "What does it look like?"

Griff scrunched up his nose in concentration. "It's hard to explain, when you can't really *see* the glass dragon. It's almost invisible," he said doubtfully. "But Lady Cavendish told me it looks like a cross between a bat and a goose."

I remembered the translucent creature that I thought I had seen flying over the meadow yesterday, with the snaking neck and bat-like wings.

I peered into the glass enclosure. All I could see

was the mist. "Are you sure it's in there?"

If the dragon had escaped, might it be to blame for Bill's missing sheep? Well, one thing I knew was that it certainly *would* be blamed if anyone discovered it was on the loose.

I wondered if I could trust Griff. After all, we hadn't know each other very long, even if he had helped me get into Direspire Hall in the first place. "I think the glass dragon has escaped," I said. "I saw it fly over my garden. It was almost invisible, but a cross between a bat and a goose sounds about right."

Griff went pale. "Are you sure?"

I nodded. "You have to tell Lady Cavendish. She needs to know that one of her creatures is loose; I can't risk the glass dragon eating any sheep, or cows." *Or people.* I couldn't risk Pa and the other farmers taking matters into their own hands either. "It's really important."

"Lady Cavendish would have a fit if she knew I'd shown you her creatures!" Griff hopped from one foot to the other in a nervous jig. "This was a really bad idea. You have to leave, Cora, please!"

A squawk, and the great big macaw sailed low overhead, narrowly missing our heads by a feather's breath. Again, I was struck by how colourful the bird was.

"Griff! Are you there?" an unfamiliar voice called out. "Come here at once. The fireplace in the library needs to be swept and refuelled."

Griff gripped my arm. "It's Mr Johnson." He pulled me towards a thicket of leafy shrubs. "You have to hide!"

But it was too late.

"And who," said a stern voice, "might you be?"

Chapter 6
Lady Cavendish

I couldn't speak. The words seethed in my head like angry bees.

It was the man from the market, the one with the injured arm, only ... Puzzled, I stared at him. Neither of his arms were in a sling. He was standing with his hands on his hips.

"Her name's Cora!" Griff appeared from behind me.

"And why is Cora here?" Mr Johnson narrowed his eyes.

Mr Johnson looked like a grumpy badger. Unlike at the market, he was now dressed in a black-and-white uniform, although the jacket was dusty and the shirt was yellowing with age. His black hair was smoothed to one side and on his face was a look of disgust, as if he'd caught me pilfering his pockets red-handed.

"She wanted to see the creatures," Griff said, ashen-faced. "It's my fault. I told her she could climb over the wall and jump on to the old woodshed."

"How long have you both been sneaking around in the glasshouse?" Mr Johnson's voice was shrill, as brittle and breakable as a thin layer of ice. It warned me to tread carefully. "Have you been meddling with the enclosures?"

"We only looked at the creatures, we didn't do anything else." Griff's voice wobbled. "But – but we think the glass dragon has escaped! Cora said she saw it fly over her garden."

Mr Johnson went a curious shade of red and his eyes bulged. "You let the glass dragon escape!"

NO! I wanted to shout. *That wasn't us!* But I couldn't.

Mr Johnson grabbed the neck of my jumper in a painful twist.

"You're in big trouble, I'll tell you that now," he hissed.

I kicked out, but Mr Johnson side-stepped, quick as a cat.

He marched me out of the glasshouse and hauled

me up the path, back towards the gates of Direspire Hall, firing questions at me all the while. "What are you doing here? Have you come to spy? Steal?"

In my fright, all my words stuck together in a lump. I couldn't speak.

"I shall take you to Lady Cavendish," he said. "And she won't be happy to hear you've been setting her precious creatures loose."

Griff followed close behind, gnawing on his raggedy thumbnail.

The fountain came into view, and with it, the entrance to Direspire itself: a wooden door with a grinning gargoyle for a door knocker.

Mr Johnson shoved me up the stone staircase, towards the doors. He stopped and looked at Griff.

"You've caused enough trouble for one day, Griff. Why don't you make yourself scarce and dismantle the old woodshed? I don't want any more uninvited visitors hopping over the wall."

Then, he heaved open the door to Direspire and pulled me inside. The door banged shut behind us, leaving Griff outside.

Inside, the dark was disorientating. I blinked to adjust my eyes to the gloom.

To my surprise, the space was piled high with

stuff, from the floor to the ceiling.

Tables were almost hidden under wooden boxes and chairs that were stacked up on each other, their legs and arms entangled. Precarious book towers and mountains of linen stood side by side. Newspapers slid in a landslide across the wooden floor. Clocks on the walls ticked out of time with each other. A large cabinet spanned one wall, lined with china dolls, their dusty eyes half-asleep and half-watchful.

Huge paintings of dour-faced people hung on the walls, all wearing uncomfortable-looking clothes and holding weasel-looking creatures.

A bell began to ring insistently.

"What the devil is going on, Arthur?" said a faint voice. It came from upstairs, from a room to the left of the upper hallway.

We followed the bell and came to a half-open door. Mr Johnson knocked.

"Come along, stop dawdling," came the impatient reply. "I haven't got time to waste."

Mr Johnson let go of my jumper and gave me a shove towards the centre of the room.

"I found this one in the glasshouse, snooping around the creatures, your ladyship. She unbolted the enclosure and the glass dragon escaped. Heavens knows what more damage she might have caused had I not caught her in time." Mr Johnson fluffed himself up like a rooster, his round, pale face smug.

My legs turned marshmallow-soft and I struggled to stand upright.

Here she was. The mysterious Lady Cavendish of Direspire Hall.

The study was dark and musty. The single window was clouded by dust; it made my throat itch just to look at it. It was a large room, but everything in it made it seem small. Just like the entrance hall, the room was stuffed full of clutter. Tables and chairs and dolls and bundles of newspapers held together with twine. Clocks that all ticked to their own time.

And then there were the paintings. Great big paintings covered the walls, the same three faces over and over again, faces that smiled, and frowned and laughed. A man, a woman and a young girl, all with fierce black eyes that followed you across the room.

Against the far wall, there was a huge wooden desk, piled high with leather-bound books and scrunched-up paper. One solitary lamp spilled orange light in the gloom.

The woman sitting at the desk tore her attention away from a sketchbook, which she snapped shut before I could glimpse her work.

"Who are you?" Her voice was sharp, each word a snap of a pencil. "What are you doing here?"

The woman in the room looked nothing like the person I imagined. I'd always thought Lady Cavendish would be regal, like a queen, or at least wearing fancy clothes. Her dark hair was cut short and brushed back, with flashes of grey around her temples, like wings. With bright, bird-like eyes she scowled at me. She wore an oversized shirt with large pockets, which held a number of pens, paintbrushes and even a book. Her trousers were also covered in pockets, and were held up by red braces. Her shirt had inkblots seeping out of the pockets, like blue bloodstains. It made me feel more at ease.

She reminded me of Wildling crow. She had the same glint in her dark eyes, a no-nonsense kind of clever.

Lady Cavendish put down her pen. She made a steeple with her fingers and I noticed cuts on her hands, and a laceration on one forearm that had bruised up yellow and green.

"Has the cat got your tongue?" Lady Cavendish snapped at me. "Child, who are you and what do you want?"

Like Wildling, the woman was ill-tempered and snippy.

Of all the times to lose my voice, this was one of the worst. *Just imagine she is Wildling crow.* I told myself. *You can talk to Wildling, can't you?*

I wriggled the letter out of my pocket. I stepped closer, holding the letter up like a white flag. Lady Cavendish snatched the letter, glanced at it quickly, then looked up at me.

"This is addressed to Mr Erwood. Is that your father? It seems the likeliest way you've managed to get hold of it."

I nodded. "I'm Cora," I squeezed out in a whisper.

Lady Cavendish studied me, not saying another word.

Mr Johnson spoke up again. "I caught her snooping around the menagerie, Lady Cavendish. I was too late to stop her releasing the dragon."

It's not true, it wasn't me. Please, give me a chance to explain, I willed Lady Cavendish. She narrowed her eyes at me, as if listening to my silence.

"Is this true?" Lady Cavendish asked me. "Has my glass dragon escaped?"

I couldn't lie; that part was true. I gave a small nod.

To my relief, she asked another question. "And were you the one who let the glass dragon escape?"

I shook my head so vigorously, I felt dizzy.

Lady Cavendish considered me for another moment that stretched uncomfortably into an additional second. Then she pushed back her chair and stood.

"First things first. Let's see if my glass dragon is indeed missing."

Chapter 7
The Call of a Glass Dragon

As we followed Lady Cavendish back to the glasshouse, I noticed Mr Johnson seemed jittery, wiping his forehead with his handkerchief. On top of the fact that his injuries from the market had mysteriously disappeared, I decided that Mr Johnson was one to watch. I didn't trust him, not one bit.

Griff was nowhere to be seen.

When we came to the glass dragon enclosure, the door was unlocked and swung open at a push. Inside, mist from the steam machine hissed and puffed, but nothing else moved.

Lady Cavendish swore under her breath, confirming the glass dragon's escape. She examined the lock. "Arthur, do you have the keys?"

Mr Johnson patted his pocket and produced a heavy set of keys, then handed them over to Lady Cavendish. I thought he hesitated before he did so. I eyed him narrowly and he glared at me with such a look of contempt that I drew in a sharp breath.

"Thank you, Arthur." Lady Cavendish pocketed the keys. "That will be all."

"Excuse me, your ladyship?" Mr Johnson frowned.

"That will be all, Arthur. Go and make yourself a cup of tea and take inventory of ... something," she said impatiently. "I'm sure you're being overcharged for the eggs and milk." She wafted her hand at him. "That's an order."

Mr Johnson gawped at me, as if it was my fault he'd been dismissed. Then he turned and stalked away, his hands clenched against his sides.

Lady Cavendish turned to me.

"I have been rather busy recently, with a project that has consumed every drop of my energy and time."

I glanced at the scratches on her hands and wondered if they had something to do with the project she was working on.

"I haven't been able to keep up with the care of

the creatures. That's why I have been looking for a creature keeper." She drummed her fingers on the glass of the dragon enclosure. "Arthur has been here for years and we have Griff, but aside from them I haven't had any luck getting people to work at Direspire Hall. I sent letters advertising for the role, but no one has taken me up on it."

That's because everyone is too scared to work here.

Except me. I wanted the role more than I'd ever wanted anything before. I just needed to convince Lady Cavendish that I was the right person for the job.

Lady Cavendish scowled at the glass enclosure. "Arthur was meant to be looking after the creatures these last few days and now the dragon has escaped, flown off to who knows where," she growled. "This is a right mess."

I had a thought. Maybe there was a way that I could help.

I spun around and headed towards the entrance. Lady Cavendish wasn't far behind.

We hurried outside into the grounds. If the glass dragon was close to Direspire Hall, maybe it would be close enough to hear me call. Thinking back to when I'd been sitting in the meadow, I tried to recall the sound the dragon had made as it passed overhead. The haunting cry had been wistful, as if it was waiting for a reply. I had spent so many years mimicking birdcalls that I could pluck the notes out of my memory like daisies, rearranging them until they fit together in a chain.

I took a deep breath, put two fingers in my mouth and whistled as loud as I could. I mimicked the shriek, which had sounded like waves of birdsong, and had made my stomach plummet as the song dipped over and over again. Up and down. Up and down.

Whhhheetwoooooohweettweetwoohwoohweeeeet

I stopped, my fingers numb.

"Do that again, girl," Lady Cavendish commanded. Her sharp eyes were fixed on me.

So I did. I whistled the glass dragon song, over and over again, not knowing if it would be heard by the creature or not. It was the only thing that worked with Wildling crow and even then, he only listened half the time.

A sudden gasp from Lady Cavendish and I stopped.

"Look over there!" Lady Cavendish said.

Sure enough, the whisper of a shape glided on to the grass, not far from where I stood. The translucent shape was difficult to make out, unless you looked to the side of it, where you could just discern an outline. Out of the corner of my eye, I could see the bat-winged and long-necked creature as it waddled up to me.

"I've never been able to mimic its call, not like that." Lady Cavendish bent down and held out her hand to the glass dragon. The creature stretched out its long neck and sniffed at her hand, then Lady Cavendish reached down and picked it up.

I followed as Lady Cavendish carried the glass dragon back to into the glasshouse and its enclosure. I longed to reach out and stroke its neck, but I held back. I knew that I had to introduce myself properly to the creature first.

At the enclosure, Lady Cavendish let the glass dragon go and locked the door firmly behind her.

The mist swirled in a serpentine shape as the dragon passed through. I pressed my hands to the glass, relieved. My idea had worked. So why did I feel so hollow? But I knew why. I felt as if I had somehow tied myself to these creatures – to the glass dragon, the seacat, the pangolin and the moonbirds – and to leave now, to sever the thread, would be unbearable.

"What did you say your name was?" Lady Cavendish asked. "Cora?"

I nodded.

Lady Cavendish glanced at me. "Come with me, Cora."

"I've been the creature keeper of Direspire Hall for almost all my life, Cora," she said. "It has given me great joy, to be the warden of these extraordinary creatures." She stopped outside the seacat's enclosure and shook her head. "I have let things slide here and it pains me to see these creatures so neglected. It proves how necessary it is to have someone take over the role of creature keeper."

She tipped her head at me, as if weighing something up, before she continued. "My late mother and father were explorers. They travelled the world, collecting creatures, which they brought back here, to Direspire Hall. I grew into the role of keeper of the creatures they left behind."

She came to the moonbird enclosure and stopped. "Do you think they are extraordinary?"

I nodded. Of course I thought they were extraordinary. Who wouldn't?

"Arthur, my butler, was keen to try his hand at creature-keeping duties, but…" Lady Cavendish shook her head. "I do not think he is suitable. You have shown great promise, bringing my glass dragon back, but it is a role that will require courage, ingenuity and an understanding of animals."

She paused. "Do you think you will make a good creature keeper?"

Yes! There was nothing I wanted more.

"Well, do you?" Lady Cavendish spoke impatiently.

"I know how to look after all sorts of creatures," I managed to say. "I've always been good with animals and birds. I grew up on a farm with cows and chickens."

Lady Cavendish laughed. "My creatures are extraordinary. They are not simple livestock."

I ploughed on, knowing that this was my only chance. "I think all creatures are extraordinary, from cats and cows to crows." I thought of Crabbit and Bella and Wildling, all special in their own way. "I can look after those creatures and I can look after yours."

The conviction in my voice shook me. I couldn't quite believe it was me speaking, but I knew more than anything that if I didn't say something, this chance would pass me by.

Lady Cavendish smiled. "Then, Cora, I will need you to start immediately." It all felt so quick. One moment I was an intruder, the next I was working for Lady Cavendish. Where was the catch?

Lady Cavendish continued. "You will be paid, of course." She mentioned a wage that made my toes curl. It would easily pay for a whole winter's worth of hay and fix the thatch on our cottage. I couldn't wait to tell Ma and Pa. They'd be angry at first, I knew, but once I explained what it meant, surely they would understand. They might even be happy.

"If you want the role, you will be required to live at Direspire Hall for a couple of weeks, at the very least, so that you can grow accustomed to the routine. You can inform your family by letter," Lady Cavendish said. "Coming and going is not allowed. To keep the creatures safe, the gates of Direspire Hall must be kept locked at all times. Only Mr Johnson has the keys to Direspire Hall, so that he can collect the weekly shop and so forth. Do you understand?"

There was the catch.

Lady Cavendish was asking me to give up seeing my ma and pa for the summer. I wouldn't be allowed to visit Bella, or Crabbit, or Wildling crow.

I felt torn. Even though I had often felt the call for adventure, the thought of not being able to go back, even to say goodbye, made my heart ache. And yet from the moment I stepped into the glasshouse, a part of me knew that my life had forever changed. I couldn't be the same person I was on the farm. Not any more.

Once you had purred at a seacat and stepped over a tortoise, called to a glass dragon and seen moonbirds fly, there was no going back. I wasn't going to say no.

Chapter 8

Instructions on Creature Keeping

The rest of the day passed in a blur.

Lady Cavendish wrote a letter to my parents, suggesting a trial apprenticeship over the summer holidays, along with a cheque for my first week's wages. "It is only fair that you are given an advance on your earnings, as you have already brought my glass dragon back," she said. She sealed the letter with wax and handed it to Mr Johnson with a stern warning that she would need a written acknowledgment from my parents that the letter had been received.

It was all very real, with no turning back now.

After that, Lady Cavendish introduced me to the creatures in the glasshouse one by one, while I trotted after her, trying to keep up. I was thankful that I'd remembered to bring my notebook with me. I scribbled down everything. I didn't want to miss something important.

"Let's start with how to feed them, shall we?" Lady Cavendish gestured over the walled enclosure, where Griff had already told me the pangolin lived. I wondered how he was getting on demolishing the woodshed, and hoped he wasn't in too much trouble for helping me into Direspire Hall.

"Focus, Cora!" Lady Cavendish snapped her fingers at me and I blushed, pushing thoughts of Griff to the back of my mind.

"A pangolin is an extraordinary creature, as rare as a diamond and just as precious." Lady Cavendish's eyes were bright. "She wears a suit of golden armour and curls up in an orb when she feels threatened. The pangolin feeds on grubs, beetles and worms, which she slurps up with a tongue as long as she is."

A golden creature that could transform into an orb? I couldn't wait to get a glimpse of her. I scribbled down *grubs, beetles and worms*.

As we walked, Lady Cavendish pointed out the large beautiful bird that watched us from the cherry trees. "The macaw is a clever bird, capable of mimicking human words. *Fascinating creature.* He eats seeds, millet, grains and nuts. Scatter them about so he can forage and find his own food. He likes apples."

Feeding the macaw sounded like feeding the chickens at home, although from the way the macaw was glaring at me, he might need some convincing that I could be trusted. I scribbled down: *Make friends with the macaw by bringing him apples.*

Lady Cavendish paused at the glass enclosure.

"Now, the moonbirds. They are trickier." Lady Cavendish tapped the glass with her fingernail, causing the birds to erupt silently off their perches. "They drink moonlight. Nothing else."

I paused, with my pencil hovering above the paper.

"Every full moon, you'll need to collect the moonlight in a copper bowl of water. There's one hanging up in the food store in the glasshouse." Lady Cavendish spoke as if it was perfectly normal to feed birds moonlight from a copper bowl. "Take the copper bowl outside the glasshouse and collect the moonlight on the surface of the water. Swirl the water clockwise. They only need feeding once a month."

This was all so wonderful and strange. The more I found out about the creatures, the more I wanted to know. Where did the moonbirds come from? Who built the glasshouse?

I opened my mouth to ask more questions, but Lady Cavendish carried on, marching towards the glass dragon enclosure. "The glass dragon gets all its nutrients from the clouds, so make sure you keep the steam machine running. To produce the clouds that the glass dragon needs, you will require leaves from the whistling trees, in the gated garden. The leaves smoulder when they fall, producing the nutritious clouds that are necessary to keep the glass dragon healthy. Griff will instruct you on how to gain access to the garden."

The smouldering leaves of the whistling trees! I'd finally uncovered the source of the constant haze that hung over Direspire Hall.

I jotted down the instructions as fast as I could, my pencil flying across the paper. *Whistling trees, gated garden, steam machine.* It all sounded rather complex, and I worried that I was going to make a mess of it. There was no time to worry about it, though. Lady Cavendish had already moved on.

I caught up with her in front of the seacat's

enclosure. "The seacat eats fish. Only fish. You'll find plenty in the ice house." Stepping away from the enclosure, Lady Cavendish spoke urgently, "Be warned, the seacat's claws are tipped with venom, much like certain types of jellyfish. One swipe and you're done for. Never let the seacat out, under any circumstances. He is a vicious, cruel beast."

Glancing up at Lady Cavendish, I was surprised by the expression on her face. Her brow was furrowed with tension. "Shall we move on?" she said.

She turned and began to stalk down the brick path. For a moment, I met the emerald eyes of the seacat, who blinked at me before slipping under the stagnant waters of his pool. I wrote down *vicious, cruel beast* in my notebook, then added a question mark, before running to catch up with Lady Cavendish.

It was late evening by the time Lady Cavendish had finished instructing me on the creatures' care, as well as the butterflies and the tortoises that roamed free in the glasshouse.

It was only when I yawned for the third time in a row that Lady Cavendish glanced at her watch. "I didn't realize the time. I'll call Arthur to show you up to your room, then I'd like for you to report to me first thing tomorrow morning. Is that understood?"

I clutched the full notebook to my chest and smiled my weary agreement. I was afraid that if I nodded, all the new and wonderful information might fall out.

It was dark by the time Lady Cavendish dismissed me, and Mr Johnson showed me to the attic room, carrying a tray with a plate of jam sandwiches and a mug of hot cocoa on it, the first food I'd been offered all day. My stomach growled.

He opened the door and flicked the light switch. The light buzzed then flickered into a dull, orange glow.

I'd been half-expecting the room to be as full of clutter as the rest of the house seemed to be, but it was sparse. Only a metal bedframe and a mattress stood in the middle of it, with the moonlight pooling through the window. The wind wolf-howled and rattled the tiles with the full force of the moor gales.

"Let's see how long you last, *creature keeper.*" Mr Johnson put the tray on the bedside table and turned on his heel to leave.

Didn't he have his hand in a sling when I saw him at the market? It looked all right now.

Mr Johnson reached for the door with the hand that had been bandaged and slammed it shut behind him.

I listened to his footsteps retreating down the creaking stairs. I didn't want to dwell on the butler's mysterious vanishing injures now. Instead, I took a look around the attic room.

The only other furniture in the room, besides the bed, was a trunk. I heaved it open. Inside, there were blankets and pillows. I scooped them up and wrapped myself in them, like a cocoon, before switching the light off and scurrying to the bed. I nibbled on the sandwiches, which didn't taste nearly as nice as Ma's homemade jam, and gulped down the cocoa.

The lumps in the mattress dug into my back and it smelled funny. Like mice. The blanket was itchy, the wool wasn't soft like the blankets Ma made. Nothing in this place fitted me properly. It was too big and too loud and too scratchy.

A loud groan made me sit up straight. I swung my legs over the side of the bed.

Under my bare feet, I felt the floorboards

shudder. A groan rumbled through the boards, as if the house was turning over in its sleep. The groan stretched into a wail, that sounded less like an old house noise and more like the animal sounds I recognized from the moor.

"Hello?" I croaked into the darkness.

In the moonlight that shone through the window, the attic room looked like another planet, full of shapes and shadows that I still didn't recognize.

Herrrooooooooooooooooooooaaaaahhhhhooooo

"Hello?" I called out. "Anyone there?"

I jumped out of bed and tried to chase the tail of the sound, before it escaped.

Herrrooooooooooooooooooooaaaaahhhhhooooo

It was the noise from the moors, the howling that had scared Merlin and Maisie and kept me up at night! From inside Direspire Hall the noise was thunderous, loud enough to shake the boards. It seemed to be coming from the back wall of the room, furthest away from the door. There was nothing but wood panelling on the wall. Oak panels that gleamed in the soft, silvery light.

"Hello?" I whispered to the wall, feeling foolish. I waited, but the noise was only a trickle now, faint and whispery.

I pressed my hands to the wood. The panels were warm, holding the heat from the house even through the night. But there was something else in the warmth, a strange sensation. I'd felt it before, at the moonbird enclosure as I'd pressed my hands to the glass.

The feeling of something alive, like the silent moonbird song.

There was something hidden in Direspire Hall. Could it have something to do with the project that Lady Cavendish was working on? Tiredness muddled my thoughts. Right now, what I needed was sleep. Everything else would have to wait until the morning.

With the cold nipping my toes, I ran back to bed and wrapped myself under the covers. And, cocooned like that, I eventually fell asleep.

Chapter 9
Keeper of the Keys

A knock at the door jolted me out of sleep. The sun was already streaming through the window and I blinked at the unfamiliar surroundings.

"Can I come in?" came a woman's voice through the door.

I sat up groggily, fighting against the tangle of blankets.

A woman peeked into the room. Her yellow hair was a mane of curls and she had a bright, warm smile. She instantly reminded me of a friendly yellow duck that would visit our farm pond.

"I'm Bea, the housekeeper. I've heard all about you from Griff, my nosy son."

I picked at the hem of the scratchy wool blanket. My head was full of being in a strange place and now that I was up, the memory of the howling creature I'd heard last night came flooding back. *Maybe I'll get to meet the creature today*, I thought with a thrill.

"Would you like some breakfast? Lady Cavendish wants to speak to you, but I told her you would need some food in your stomach first. I've made porridge with lots of cream." Bea winked. "Come on."

I followed Bea down the rickety attic stairs. She smelled of lemons and I suddenly felt very crumpled and unwashed. I felt even more out of place in the grand, strange house than before. I wished I had Crabbit with me. Having a big orange cat by your side would make *anyone* feel braver. Today was a big day. I had to prove to Lady Cavendish that she had picked the right person for the job.

Direspire Hall had lots of twisty stairs and creaky hallways. Paintings with pale-faced people frowned, their eyes seeming to follow me.

And everywhere there were things to trip over or circle around. Boxes and furniture and papers, newspapers, and books. There seemed to be no order to anything.

"Lady Cavendish is a collector, of sorts. You'll soon get used to it." Bea picked up a footstool that blocked our path and considered where to put it for a moment, before shoving it up against the wall. The pile of empty plant pots teetered perilously next to it.

"One thing you'll quickly learn," Bea said, "is that Lady Cavendish likes things kept the way they are, which means no one is allowed to clean or clear anything without her express permission, which she rarely gives." Bea dragged her finger across the top of a dusty table and sighed. "Which makes it almost impossible to do my job."

It was such a change from our small cottage, where everything was useful and had its place. It was all very strange.

Unlike the rest of the house, the kitchen was neat and tidy. An oven warmed the room and porridge bubbled on the stove top. A blue ceramic vase held bright yellow daffodils on the windowsill. There was still dew clinging to their petals. The sun streamed through the sparkling window and the door was open to the garden. I could smell the tulips that grew wild along the path. All at once, my heart ached to see Ma and Pa and Bella and Crabbit. But I forced myself to imagine the fixed thatch, smelling sweet. A barn full of winter feed. Ma, warm and happy. Pa, smiling his rare smile. Bella, safe and well. I was doing this for them.

And I tried to think about seeing the extraordinary creatures again. The idea of learning how to care for them, of learning all about them, made my heart skip a beat.

Ma and Pa would be proud of me, even if I couldn't always get my words out right.

Bea gave me a bowl of porridge, steaming hot, with a puddle of cream in the centre. "Lady Cavendish didn't say much about where you'd come from, Cora. Only that you were here to take over creature keeping duties," she said, with a question in her voice.

I shrugged, hoping I wouldn't seem rude. Everything was so new and strange that I couldn't speak.

"Griff is out fixing the trellis in the vegetable garden." Bea handed me a mug of milky tea. "I've said that he should give you a hand later on, with the creatures. I'm sure you could use a little extra help on your first day."

I nodded. I hoped he hadn't got in too much trouble yesterday.

I had finished my porridge. "Go on, you'd better go and see Lady Cavendish now." Bea took my bowl and swiped the table clean. She pointed at the kitchen door. "Head up the stairs and to the left at the landing."

It was very quiet. Our farmhouse was never quiet, not even at night. Ma and Pa *both* snored and Crabbit was a night-time hunter, meowing and scratching and skittering as he chased after mice and moths and ghosts. I pushed away another stab of homesickness. The thrill of the day ahead was like an amulet against the feeling of homesickness.

I stopped outside the room, because I could hear voices from inside.

"She's not suitable, your ladyship. She's only a child!" It was Mr Johnson's voice. I felt a rush of anger.

"You have hardly done a good job yourself, Arthur," Lady Cavendish barked. "I was horrified to see the state the cages are in. What exactly have you been up to all this time?"

Mr Johnson spluttered in protest, but Lady Cavendish continued. "I will hear no more on the matter. Cora appears more than capable. I don't have the time to care for the creatures in the way they deserve, and you clearly don't either."

"I beg that you listen to me, your ladyship!" Mr Johnson sounded exasperated. "Nothing good can come from any of this. Only *weeks* ago you decided to bring two complete strangers to Direspire Hall, who arrived in the dead of night, and now you've decided to hire a child to look after dangerous creatures. Have we not always managed perfectly fine?"

"I'm thankful for your service all these years. But the role of creature keeper has been given to Cora. That's the end of it."

"I hope you won't regret that decision."

"Is that a threat?" Lady Cavendish's voice rose sharply.

"More of a warning, your ladyship," Mr Johnson demurred. "I've been working at Direspire Hall since your parents were alive. It pains me that the responsibility of the creatures be given to a child. It's irresponsible."

"You forget that I was a child when I started looking after the creatures, not much older than Cora herself," Lady Cavendish said, sharply.

"But, Lady Cavendish," Mr Johnson persisted.

"That's enough, Arthur. Please leave now."

I stepped quickly away from the door, but it burst open.

"Have you not got enough work, girl? Sneaking around like that." Mr Johnson stormed past and down the staircase.

I pressed against the door and shouldered it open.

The room was dark, the curtains still drawn, stifling any light that might have made it through the dust. The air was thick and smelled of moths and dusty cobwebs.

"Cora, is that you?" Lady Cavendish said. "Took you long enough!"

Lady Cavendish was sitting at her desk. She nodded to a chair close by.

I battled to the chair, stepping over several boxes. I dragged the heavy chair towards the desk and balanced myself on the edge of the leather seat.

I studied Lady Cavendish, searching for the crow-like features that had made it easier to talk to her the day before. Luckily, her eyes were no less piercing and crow-like; in fact, she looked more like Wildling this morning than yesterday.

"I'm sure you have lots of questions about my unusual creatures. I am trusting you with their care." Lady Cavendish narrowed her eyes. "If you keep my trust, you will learn everything I know about creature keeping."

She handed me a bundle of keys. "These are the only set of keys for the glasshouse and the animal enclosures. After the glass dragon escape, I'd like you to keep the glasshouse locked when you're not in there. Don't lose the keys."

I pocketed the heavy keys, feeling the weight of responsibility.

"Is there anything else you'd like to ask me?"

I thought about the noises I had heard last night, the howls from inside the walls.

"Have I seen all the creatures?" I asked tentatively.

Lady Cavendish looked surprised. "Of course," she said. "I've told you everything you need to know. Please report to me any irregularities, or issues you might come across, but I expect you to follow my instructions to the letter. Is that understood? Now, go. I have some painting I'd like to get done today."

Lady Cavendish dismissed me with a wave of her hand.

I decided, as I closed her study door behind me, that I would ask Griff about the howls I'd heard, the same animal sounds I'd heard on the moors. Maybe he would know where they were coming from and what exactly was making the noises.

Chapter 10

The Marvellous Travelling Menagerie

Outside, the sky was blue and cloudless. A haze of insects gathered above the flower beds. I loved the smell of the earth after a storm.

I hurried along the path that skirted around the building, eager to see the creatures again. My pulse quickened as the glasshouse came into view.

The glittering dome was exactly as I remembered it, the sunlight splintering off the panes. Once inside, I pulled off my wool jumper. The early morning sun beamed through the glass panes, heating up the steamy air. There was a strong smell from the lilies and the heavy tangy smell from the fruit trees.

Following the path, I found the glass enclosure, where the moonbirds were kept. Behind the glass, the moonbirds were awake and fluttering from branch to branch. They pecked at the dirt below the branches, flipping over dead leaves and tiny pebbles.

I pressed my hands to the glass and felt the same vibrations that I'd noticed the day before. The reckless and curious part of me longed to open the door to the enclosure and hear the birdsong, even if it meant my ears popped and I never heard anything else again.

"Cora!" Griff appeared along the path and gave me a wide grin.

"So, you're the new creature keeper? How did you manage that!" He laughed. "I was sure you were going to get kicked out of the gates when I saw the look on Mr Johnson's face."

I couldn't help laughing with him. "I don't think Mr Johnson is happy I'm still here." I told Griff about helping Lady Cavendish bring the glass dragon home.

"Wow, you really can talk to animals!" Griff gazed at me admiringly. "Where did you learn that?"

"I can't really talk to them." I paused, wondering how to best explain it. "It's more like ... listening to them, I suppose, and sort of copying them. Understanding birds and animals is much easier than trying to understand people. Creatures will never lie to you if you really listen to them."

We followed the pebble path that threaded through the glasshouse.

"Will you teach me?" Griff bounced alongside me.

I glanced at him, trying to work out whether he was serious or not. The kids at school would have laughed in my face. I shrugged. "I suppose so," I said.

From above us, the macaw flew low and landed in a cherry tree nearby. Cocking its head to the side, it fixed us with a look, watching us warily. "*Craaaaawk*!" the bird shrieked at us, bobbing his head up and down, before sending out such a shrill whistle that I winced.

I scooted into a crouch and pulled Griff down next to me. "I can show you now, but you have to do everything I say. I don't want to scare the macaw."

Griff crossed his legs and nodded, his eyes gleaming.

I sat down next to him and relaxed my shoulders, letting my hands sit in my lap, palms up, to show that I didn't have anything in my hand. No pebbles or twigs or other projectiles. "You have to show the macaw that you don't mean it any harm."

Griff copied me, wriggling into a comfortable position.

"Now," I said. "You can sing to him."

"What?" Griff said. "I can't sing!"

"Like this," I said. Pursing my lips, I whistled, mimicking the macaw's shrill whistle, with the pitch rising up, a happy tune that made me think of summer and strawberry jam, before bringing the notes down, in a soft sigh.

The macaw craned his neck and fluffed up his feathers, bobbing from one foot to the other in a way that wasn't unlike Griff. I had caught his attention.

"See? I'm singing him a happy tune so he knows that I want to be friends."

Griff took a deep breath and blew out a raspberry, startling the macaw into flapping its wings and sending me into a fit of giggles

"I'm sorry," I gasped in between snorts of laughter. "I might have to teach you how to whistle first."

Griff laughed too, then we heard another laugh join in.

We stared up at the tree.

To my delight, the macaw was laughing, his head bobbing up and down and his wings spread outwards, showing the beautiful yellow and blue feathers. He cackled loudly, stomping up and down the branch.

"I think he likes us!" Griff grinned. "Or he's making fun of us, I'm not sure which."

"He wants to be friends," I said, watching as the large bird twirled on the branch, his marvellous bright feathers shimmering in the light. I clambered back to my feet and dusted off my clothes. "He needs a name, now that we've been introduced."

"What will your name be?" I called up to the macaw.

"*Name!*" the bird screeched, making me jump. Lady Cavendish had told me that it was a mimic, but I hadn't expected it to be so quick.

"What about Bird-brain?" Griff jumped up to his feet. "Or Feather-butt?"

"*Butt, butt, butt,*" chortled the bird, copying Griff.

I considered the macaw, now chuckling quietly and still peering down at us with one beady eye.

"I think Echo is a good name." I called to the bird. "What do you think? Do you like Echo?"

"*Echo!*" cackled the bird, which sent both Griff and me into another fit of giggles.

Leaving Echo chattering to himself, we carried on along the path, ducking under swaying ferns and low-hanging fruit. In some places the path was so narrow, we had to walk in single file, the spaces between the plants closing in to form an impenetrable wall.

Griff bounced ahead, his feet tripping up on the uneven path every now and then.

I was curious about him. I wondered again why I'd never seen him in town or in our classrooms. I would have noticed him, I was sure, with his wild hair and galloping gait.

"Don't you go to school?" I asked.

Griff shook his head vigorously. "I've never been to school. Ma teaches me how to read and write."

"Have you always lived at Direspire Hall?" I asked.

"No, we used to live with my pa. He owns a travelling zoo called *The Marvellous Travelling Menagerie* and we would travel the country with him and his creatures." Griff's voice trembled. "It was horrible."

"But why?" I couldn't imagine being on the road

with all kinds of different creatures as anything other than wonderful.

Griff hesitated. Then he said, "Pa used to keep Mum and me locked up in a cage while we travelled. He was afraid we would leave him."

"That *is* horrible," I said. "I'm sorry."

The path widened out and Griff fell into step with me. "My pa had a secret though. Most of the creatures he had were very ordinary, but he tricked people into thinking they were extraordinary. He had a donkey painted in black-and-white stripes that he called a zebra, and a chicken he said could predict the future, that always ended up in the pot after the show and got replaced with another one. He tied a horn to a horse and called it a unicorn." Griff snorted. "They were just what he called *fillers*. He only had one creature that was extraordinary. Pa bought it on the underground market for extraordinary creatures, where it had been smuggled across the seas on a shipping boat. He traded it for every penny our family had. He called it the Great Crustacean!

"It could *expand* its jaws and crunch down anything, grinding down the bones." Griff shuddered. "The audience were always amazed and would *cheer* when Pa unveiled the creature," he said bitterly. "But it gave me nightmares, knowing that we were living with something that could eat me up in one gulp. When I was little, Pa would threaten to feed me to the creature if I ever stepped out of line." Griff blinked rapidly.

I imagined a smaller version of Griff, being told he would be thrown to a ravenous creature. "How awful," I managed, but it didn't feel nearly enough. "Where is your pa now?"

Griff hesitated, then said, "Brambury Town."

Brambury. That was only a few miles away from here.

Only then did I notice that someone else was here in the glasshouse with us. Half-hidden behind a rose bush, Mr Johnson snipped at the flowers with pruning shears, gathering a bouquet of blood-red blooms. I'd left the door to the glasshouse unlocked. His frown twisted unpleasantly when he caught me watching him. How had I not noticed him there? The butler was awfully quiet on his feet.

"Mr Johnson's keeping an eye on us," I whispered to Griff. "We'd better move along."

We stopped on the bridge across the pond and peered down into the water.

Griff spit-balled into the pond, sending ripples across the surface. A shadow skulked under a lily pad and I shivered. The perch were circling just under the water's surface.

Once we were across the pond, we reached a small hut, tucked up against the glass wall. This was the storage hut. The door was padlocked, but I found the key on the bundle that Lady Cavendish had given me.

I opened the door. The smell of mouldy hay hit me first. Damp and dusty. My eyes adjusted to the gloom, until I could make out shelves and shelves of tins and baskets and bundles of straw. It was a mess. A mouse zipped out of a crack in a wooden barrel, where seeds were spilling on to the floor.

I cracked the barrel open. Inside was filled to the brim with nuts and seeds. I recognized the golden ears of millet and stripy sunflower seeds.

There was another barrel that made a strange rustling noise, like dry leaves being scrunched up in your hand. Inside, thousands of white and yellow wriggling bodies. Grubs.

"You must be for the pangolin," I said to the bucket. "I'll be back for you later."

I filled a tin bucket full of seeds and brought it outside.

The air was heating up in the glasshouse. The smell reminded me of the fields after a summer storm, earthy and green. Or Maisie when she rolled in fresh cut grass. I hoped she had made it back to Bill after fleeing with Merlin the night before.

We spread the seeds and millet heads around the spot where we had last seen Echo, who had disappeared somewhere else. I listened out for him, but the glasshouse was quiet, apart from the rustle of softly moving leaves.

I had the strange feeling that we were being watched, even though I saw no sign of Mr Johnson. Yet the prickling sensation remained, and I caught myself turning around, as if I could catch the watcher. But there was nothing except me and Griff and the butterflies that fluttered endlessly all around us.

Stopping at the pangolin enclosure, I peered in, hoping to see the creature, but the sandy enclosure was quiet.

I'll come back tonight, I thought. It was nocturnal, after all.

The seacat's enclosure gave out a reek that was

sharp and cat-like. The smell was like a paper-cut on the inside of my nose; it stung and made me wince.

Emerald eyes glared at me from the stagnant pond.

"The pond is filthy," I said. "I'm going to have to clean it as soon as possible."

"Mr Johnson was supposed to be keeping the enclosures clean while Lady Cavendish looked for a creature keeper, but he didn't do a very good job." Griff stood behind me, looking fearfully into the seacat enclosure. "Are you sure you want to go in there?" Griff shivered. "How are we going to get the seacat out of the way?"

"I'll find a way. We're going to have to clean out the enclosure, one way or another!" I said. "It can't be very nice living in such a messy cage."

The large cat made a very strange twittering noise, like a sparrow.

Chhhirrrrrrrrrrriiiiiipppppppp

I imitated the sound back to him, whistling through my teeth.

"What was that?" Griff said. "Do it again!"

I scanned his face to see if he was making fun of me, but he was just looking at me with great interest.

I whistled again.

Chhhirrrrrrrrrriiiiiipppppppppppp

The seacat drifted from one side of the murky pond to the other, leaving a trail of silt in its wake. Back and forth, then around in a circle. Crabbit would never walk around in circles; it wasn't natural. A cat of any kind should have the space to stalk, to run and to play.

The enclosure was too small, I realized. Such a large animal needed more space, more than the glasshouse could provide.

It was all very well keeping cows and chickens on a farm, where they had space to graze and scratch and play with their own kind. But would an extraordinary wild creature like the seacat ever be content to stay confined?

I hadn't thought about how it would feel to care for animals who perhaps shouldn't be caged at all; I had only thought how lucky I was to be around such extraordinary creatures. Troubled, I decided to work on the things I could control. And that meant making sure I was doing everything in my power for the creatures in my care.

The enclosure was made up of two areas. One larger area had the pond in which the seacat was currently submerged, and the other appeared to be the sleeping area.

"Is that where you sleep?" I asked the eyes in the pond. There was an ammonia-like odour from the entrance to the box. Peering closer, I noticed a sliding door over the entrance hole that looked like it was operated by a lever. I drummed my fingers on the metal bars, as a plan began to form, as to how we could clean the enclosure without losing an arm or a leg.

"Don't worry," I said to the seacat. "We're going to come in and clean up."

Griff sucked in a deep breath. "I'm not sure that's a good idea. What if it grabs us with its webbed claws? Or chews us to pieces?"

"I'm the creature keeper, Griff," I reminded him, "and looking after creatures means you have to make sure they have a clean environment to live in." I thought of Bella and her soft, sweet-smelling barn and the grassy field where the herd grazed.

Using a wheelbarrow from the food store, I trucked over a stack of hay and a spade, while Griff headed to the cold store room in search of fish, to use as bait.

Griff bounced back to the enclosure, carrying a huge rainbow trout.

"If we can trap the seacat in the sleeping area, out of the way, we'll be able to clean the main enclosure." I pointed to the area of the enclosure where the seacat slept. It had a door that could be opened or closed from the outside.

Taking the trout from Griff, I threw it through the bars of the sleeping area, where it landed with a thump on the damp straw.

Come on, seacat. Climb out of the pond and go and eat your breakfast.

I chirruped at the seacat again, in a way that I hoped might be encouraging.

Chhhirrrrrrrrrrriiiiiippppppppppppp

The seacat flicked its ears in my direction. Then he slunk out of the water and snuffled curiously towards his sleeping pen, his lips pulled back from dagger-like incisors. The creature was far larger than I'd realized, bigger than any dog I'd ever seen. He snuffled at the entrance to the sleeping area, picking up on the smell of fresh fish. Cautiously, the large cat slunk into the enclosed space.

"Quick, the lever!" I hissed to Griff.

Griff wound the lever around and around. With a clatter, the door to the sleeping area slammed shut. Apart from a flick of his ears, the seacat barely registered that he'd been locked inside, so intent was he on devouring the trout.

With the seacat secured in the sleeping area, I unlocked the door to the main enclosure, with the bunch of keys that Lady Cavendish had given me.

After a moment of hesitation, Griff ventured in with me. With spades and the wheelbarrow, Griff and I went about clearing the enclosure of the build-up of dung and fish bones. It was gruelling work, and soon my dungarees were covered in reeking mud.

Then, we went and dug up some small saplings from the garden and put them into large pots and brought them into the enclosure, so that the seacat would have some shade from the bright sunlight.

Finally, it was time to clean out the murky pond.

"Where are we going to get seawater from, to fill

it back up?"

"We'll have to collect it from the deep well," Griff said, with a pained expression. "It's my least favourite place in Direspire. It gives me nightmares."

Griff heaved up the wheelbarrow. "Come on," he said. "Let's get it over with."

Chapter 11
The Deep Well

Griff pushed the wheelbarrow around the glasshouse and through the orchard. As we passed the last of the trees, I spotted a large round wooden cover on the ground.

Griff stopped the wheelbarrow by the well. "Lady Cavendish told me that if you fall down it, it'll take you all the way to the middle of the earth. That's what she said, probably to scare me." Griff shivered. "And I guess it worked."

Together, we hauled the wooden covering off the well. The boards were old and crumbled slightly under my fingers. As well as a whiff of the sea, I could smell something else from the hollow. Like rotten eggs and mildew. It turned my stomach.

Griff passed me an old metal bucket, with a thick

rope tied to the end of it. "You can use this to collect the water, but I'm standing way back. I don't want to fall in." He jiggled nervously on the spot.

The bucket seemed to take for ever to reach the bottom and even longer to pull back up, but finally I was able to start filling the wheelbarrow. Clumps of green seaweed floated in the bottom of the barrow by the time I'd filled it to the brim.

Heaving the cover back on top of the well, I felt a sudden relief. The smell of rot and damp had given me a dull headache, and I couldn't wait to get away from it.

Inside the glasshouse, we refilled the pond with the fresh seawater. The enclosure was ready.

Locking the door behind us, I wound the lever up, opening the door between the two enclosures. With a growl, the big cat padded into the main enclosure and sniffed his newly clean home.

I watched him, marvelling. The seacat's stripes were sea-blue and midnight black. He walked awkwardly, without the grace of Crabbit, as if unsure of the steadiness of the ground beneath his feet. He slunk into the pond and, seemingly content, disappeared under the surface with half-closed eyes, until he was only a shadow under the water.

Now for the sleeping area. After winding the lever down once more, securing the seacat in the main enclosure, I unlocked the door to the sleeping area and stepped into the dark box, gagging at the pungent smell. Underfoot, the hay was slimy with mud and rot. No creature should live like this.

Using the spades, we quickly shovelled out the reeking hay. After years of cleaning out Bella and the herd stalls, I fell into a rhythm and the small area was soon clear. I grabbed handfuls of clean hay and scattered it on the floor.

Finally, the cage was clean. I locked the door to the sleeping area and wound the lever up, allowing the creature to go back and forth freely between the two spaces.

From the pond, all I could see were his emerald eyes, two bright spots watching us curiously. "I wonder what he's thinking?" I said to Griff. "Do you think he looks happier, now the enclosure is clean?" I couldn't stop comparing the pond to the life the cat would have lived, swimming free in the open sea.

For a moment, Griff gazed into the cage, as if he hadn't heard me. Then he said, "I don't feel as afraid of the big blue cat now, not after I've spent hours scrubbing his poop off the floor."

"We can't just call him *the big blue cat*, he needs a name." I studied the eyes above the waterline. Once, a huge storm had swept across the moors and almost destroyed our barn, with all our cows inside. Pa had called the windstorm a "tempest" from the sea, and said that we should never underestimate the weather. We were lucky our cows were safe, but I never forgot the storm that had blown through.

"I'm going to call him Tempest," I said to Griff. "He's got wild, stormy eyes of the sea." I thought the name suited him well.

Together, we walked out of the glasshouse. I was pleased how well the day had gone so far; nothing had gone disastrously wrong.

Suddenly, Bea appeared from around the grey building. "Cora, there's someone for you at the gates!" Her face was drained of colour. "He's threatening to tear down Direspire Hall to find you. You'd better go quick, before Arthur and Lady Cavendish hear him!"

Chapter 12

Bear at the Gates

I could hear Pa's yelling from all the way up the path.

My feet flew over the paving, my heart in my mouth.

Merlin whinnied at the sight of me. And there, holding his reins, was my pa, all bear-shaped and furious.

I leaped at the gate and he caught me in a fierce hug. The bars of the gate dug into my ribcage, but I didn't care. I only cared that he was here.

It was also a huge relief to see that Merlin had made it home safely.

"You had your ma and me worried half to death," Pa growled, releasing me at last. "What were you thinking, Cora? We didn't know what had happened – when we woke up and your bed was empty, when Merlin came home on his own. And then the letter arrived . . . Cora, what were you thinking?"

"Pa, did you get the money?" I said.

Pa passed his hand through his hair. "The money isn't important, Cora. You need to come home. It isn't safe here."

"The money *is* important, Pa. And I need to be here. I can be useful, *really* useful. I'm learning to look after lots of different creatures. They need me. I know that Bella and the herd will be all right with you and Ma . . . You'll have enough money to keep Bella now, won't you?"

Pa gave a reluctant nod. "The cheque from Lady Cavendish was more than enough to cover the cost of keeping her."

"Then I want to stay," I said firmly.

I need to stay, is what I really wanted to say. It was difficult to describe, but for the first time I didn't feel out of place. I felt like I belonged here, with the other odd creatures, including Griff.

Pa shook his head. "The answer is no, Cora. You're coming home now." He rattled at the iron bars. "How do you get these blasted gates open?"

I braced my heart and took a big gulp of air. "Lady Cavendish doesn't like visitors. Pa, I'm staying here, at Direspire Hall."

Pa didn't say anything. The silence was worse than angry words.

I ploughed on. "I'm doing it for you and Ma and for the farm."

And I was doing it for myself. To learn everything I could about extraordinary creatures. To make sure they were as happy as they possibly could be.

Through gritted teeth, Pa said, "Cora, I want you to open the gate and come out. I'm taking you back to the farm. I'm taking you home."

I stepped away from the gates, a piece of my heart shattering with each step. "I'm sorry, Pa, I have to do this." Another step.

"I'm old enough to start figuring out what I want to do. Remember what Ma said, that I would find my own path?"

"This isn't what she had in mind, Cora."

"If it was what she had in mind, then it wouldn't be my path, Pa. It would be hers."

I heard a clattering of pebbles under excited feet, and turned to see Griff, with Bea in tow.

Bea put her hand on Griff's shoulder, holding him still. "Are you Cora's father?" she asked. There was an edge to her voice.

"I am indeed," Pa growled. "And who might you be?" I knew it was the fright of losing me that was stealing his manners, but I still blushed.

"Bea is the housekeeper here, Pa," I said. "She made me breakfast."

"Is that so?" Pa reluctantly passed his hand through the gate and held it out for Bea to shake. "Apologies, I've been looking for Cora. She failed to mention she was thinking of taking up a job in Direspire Hall. Her ma is beside herself with worry, as you can imagine. We only found out where she was after receiving the letter from Lady Cavendish."

Bea hesitated, then shook Pa's hand. She let go quickly and stood back, once again holding on to Griff's shoulders like he was a lifeboat and she was lost at sea.

"Cora says that she's the new creature keeper?" Pa said with a question attached. "Surely not. She's only a child."

Bea nodded. "She is, yes, and Lady Cavendish thinks she'll be a good one too. I'll be looking out for Cora while she's here. Lady Cavendish is very

kind. I'll make sure Cora doesn't get into trouble."
Bea flashed a quick smile at me.

"Please, Pa," I begged. "If I stay, there's money
to fix the roof in time for winter *and* keep Bella."
I paused. "I want to be the creature keeper of
Direspire Hall."

Pa seemed to shrink. His shoulders sagged and
the bear left his body.

"If this is what you really want, Cora."

"Yes, it is."

Pa nodded. Then he stepped forward and
whispered, too low for Bea and Griff to overhear,
"If you get into trouble, light a lamp in the highest
window. Bill will be on the look-out on the moors
and he will send word to Ma and me."

Pa brushed a hand across his eyes. "I'll head
home and tell your ma you're safe."

I swallowed the lump in my throat. "Please tell
her I love her and I'll see her in a few weeks; that's
how long Lady Cavendish said it would take to get
used to the creature keeping routine. You know
how busy it is, working with animals." I felt less
certain of staying the longer Pa was still here. "Look
after Bella for me. And Crabbit. Don't let him tease
the crows."

"I'll be back to see you in a few days' time." Pa led Merlin in a loop, then hitched up on the saddle and set off, back down the trail.

I watched them go, with an ache of sadness. This was the adventure I'd always dreamed about, but it still hurt to see him leave.

"I bet you'd both like a hot cocoa and some sandwiches for tea, isn't that right?" Bea said brightly. "I'll bring them out to the glasshouse."

"Only if I can have some of my ma's jam!" I grinned. "I've got a whole jar; I'll bring it down from the attic."

"That sounds lovely, Cora." Bea's eyes twinkled. "We can celebrate your first day with it."

Chapter 13
Through the Walls

Even though I'd grown up on a farm, where hard work was expected, I was astonished at how tired I was after taking care of the creatures of Direspire. There was so much to take in. My whole body felt as heavy as a bucketful of stones by bedtime.

After supper, I said goodnight to Griff and Bea, who made their way to the East Wing where they slept. The only lights were on the upper hallway that led to each of the wings of the house and the attic, where my bed was waiting for me. Too late, I realized I'd forgotten to ask Griff about the noises I'd heard the night before. Would they happen again tonight? I padded towards the attic.

Halfway across the upper hallway, a clatter from the foyer froze me in place.

From over the banister, I heard a hissed curse word, and a shadow stepped around a pile of boxes. Footsteps, then the door creaked open and bright moonlight spilled into the foyer. It was Mr Johnson, wearing a heavy navy overcoat and walking boots, rather than his black-and-white butler uniform. He slipped out of the house and closed the door behind him.

I wonder where he is going at this time of night? It was none of my business, and the corridor, with all the portraits gazing down at me, was making me nervous. I hurried up the stairs, taking two steps at a time, as if a ghostly dog was snapping at my heels.

In the attic, I changed into an old shirt that Bea had lent me, and I jumped into the bed.

Only minutes had passed when it started – that noise again, the same one as last night. It was a rumble, like muted thunder, but when I peered out of the window to check, the sky was clear.

Herrrooooooooooooooooooaaaaahhhhhooooo

I could feel it vibrating through the bed, as if the house had growled at some unknown threat.

In spite of my exhaustion from the day, I was

alert, adrenaline flowing through my veins. I knew there was no way I would be able to sleep without finding out what the noise was. I pulled on my dungarees and my shoes.

There it was again. The muffled roar was drawn out and mournful and sounded strangely far away and yet also as though it was coming from the room itself. I dropped to the floor and pressed my ear against the boards. The sound was clearer, but still distant. Getting back up, I dusted my knees and walked to the far wall, like I'd done on that first night.

I pressed my ear against the furthest wall from the door and listened carefully. The heavy thrum was so much clearer here that the hairs on my neck stood up.

Without thinking, I opened my mouth and pitched my voice at the same low tone.

Herrrooooooooooooooooooaaaaahhhhhooooo

To my surprise, the forlorn sound echoed back to me.

It was a creature. And it was trapped within the walls of Direspire Hall!

I began frantically knocking on the wood panels that made up the walls. If there was a creature stuck, I had to help. There must be an empty space somewhere. Could it be in the recess of a chimney? A crevasse between the bricks? Each knock gave a dull thud. I worked quickly, knocking on each panel, until far at the back of the wall, I heard a hollow sound.

With trembling fingers, I felt around for a curve in the wood and found a clasp.

A small hidden door popped open, revealing a dark space.

From inside came the smell of cellars. Cold, stale air.

I peered into the space. It was a passageway, lined with more wooden panels. I leaned further in and saw that the passageway abruptly became stairs that twisted downwards and out of sight.

I brushed my clammy hands down the side of my trousers.

Herrrooooooooooooooooooaaaaahhhhhooooo

The groan travelled up the dark passageway. That plaintive noise decided me. I grabbed my torch from my bag and took a deep breath.

I ducked into the space. Closing the door behind me, I turned on the torch, which let out a bright beam of light that shook in my trembling hand. It was like being inside a coffin. The walls closed in and I had to swallow the urge to scream. I gripped the torch tighter, using the light like a sword, slicing through the darkness.

The stairs were steep. They followed the curve of the wall and I climbed down, being careful to step quietly. Soon, I'd left the orange glow of the attic room behind in the curve of the stairwell. It felt as though I was being squeezed by the walls. Sweat beaded on my forehead.

I wish Griff was here. The thought surprised me. I found being around most people tiring, but in a few short days I'd found Griff to be different to most people I knew. He said what he meant. He might have been frightened to walk down the stairs, just like I was right now, but he wouldn't *pretend* that he wasn't afraid. It was things like that which made him easy to be around.

I reached another door in the stairs. A faint glow seeped from underneath. I gently pressed my ear against the door. A bee's hum of sound came through the wood, a scratch of pen on paper.

I wondered whether the room belonged to Lady Cavendish, picturing her behind the desk, writing under the lamp.

Holding my breath, I tiptoed away and carried on, following the stairs downwards.

Herrrooooooooooooooooooaaaaahhhhhooooo

The sound was clearer and louder. I was getting closer. Dagger-teeth and slashing claws kept appearing in my head and I had to squeeze the images out, before I lost my courage and turned back. I knew that no matter how scary, no creature deserved to be trapped behind walls, miserable and alone.

Down, down, down I went, not knowing how far I'd descended. The air grew colder and I shivered. The air smelled of damp earth and I wondered whether I'd gone so far as to be underground now. There was no way of knowing.

Suddenly, the stairs opened up into another passageway that was large enough for me to stand with plenty of room overhead. I stepped forward, sweeping the beam of the torch over the wood-panelled walls. A hallway with rooms leading off it. *How strange,* I thought. It was almost like another floor had been built beneath Direspire Hall, a network of rooms and corridors. There were lamps on the walls but I didn't dare turn them on, in case they attracted attention from upstairs. The thought of being discovered made me quicken my step. The animal roars were much closer now and seemed to be coming from the furthest door along the corridor.

I paused outside, with one hand on the handle. My heart hammered in my chest, so loud I wondered if the creature on the other side could hear it. The groans had stopped. It was quiet.

I am the creature keeper of Direspire Hall. And I have to help that creature.

I pressed down on the handle and the door swung open.

Chapter 14

The Secret Room

I swept the torchlight over the small room. It smelled briny. Like a rockpool under a hot sun. But earthy too, like soil recently turned over.

The small room held nothing but a table, with some shears on it, and a pile of gardening clippings. A jumble of roses, leaves, ivy and even a small tree. Blue daisies and pink tulips peeped out among the greenery.

I shone my torch over the heap of plants. I must have been mistaken. There wasn't anything that looked alive in the room. Nothing that would have made those worrying calls of distress.

I swung the torch back around the room once more and a movement caught my eye.

What was that? I trained the torchlight on the mound of green leaves and flowers.

The plants moved. To my horror and disbelief, the pile of leaves and flowers stirred, rising up into the air and forming the shape of an animal. An animal as large as Bella the cow.

The creature had four stubby legs, large grey ears and a long snout. Across its broad back, the plants and flowers appeared to grow right on to its skin. Right in the middle, a tree with red leaves spiralled upwards.

It was like a very small elephant, with a garden on its back.

Two wary brown eyes stared at me.

Speechless, I watched as the ferns on the creature's back stood up, like the fur on the hackles of a dog.

I took a step back, but I wasn't frightened. The creature was so strange, like nothing I could have dreamed existed, that I was afraid to look away, in case it disappeared like a dream.

I stood as still as a heron.

The creature gave a sorrowful roar that sent a shiver down my spine.

Herrroooooooooooooooooooaaaaahhhhhooooo

Such a deep booming sound, it reverberated under my feet. It was no wonder the noise travelled so far across the moors, frightening animals and people. The sonorous call was eerie, and mournful, like storm-driven waves crashing against a sea cliff.

I won't hurt you, I wanted the creature to know. *I'm a friend.*

I took a deep breath and tried to echo the creature's call.

Herrroooooooooooooooooooaaaaahhhhhooooo

It was the creature's turn to back away from me, flapping its large ears. It curved its trunk into a question mark.

It smelled of new sprung grass and crushed petals and saltwater.

Then the creature moved again, but closer this time.

From this distance, I could examine it more closely. Green moss covered its back in a soft carpet, exactly as if in the crags of a stone wall. From there, ferns unfurled in soft waves. Vines with glossy leaves curled downwards and small flowers bloomed in patches, a wildflower meadow that stretched across its shoulders. On top of it all, the small tree grew straight out of its back, its twisted branches leafy with roots dug into the moss.

It was like a walking, living garden!

The creature snorted and spun away, trotting over to the corner of the room and flopping down in a heap. Its large ears folded up against its sides and it curled its trunk around itself. Only the green, fronded ferns swayed warily from side to side, mimicking the flick of a cat's tail. At least the creature had stopped its awful sad noise.

Why was this creature being kept in a secret room below Direspire Hall? Lady Cavendish had instructed me to look after her creatures. Why not this one?

Suddenly, from outside the room, I heard footsteps.

The creature heard them too and retreated further into the corner of the room.

Quickly, I peered around the room, searching for somewhere to hide.

The table. It was the only place in the room that

could hide me. I threw myself into a slide across the floor and squeezed myself under the low table, turning off the torch not a moment too soon.

The door opened and the glow of a lamp entered the room.

"Good evening. Let's try this again, shall we?" It was Lady Cavendish.

I heard the strange creature growl. Carefully, I peered out from under the table.

Lady Cavendish stood nearby, just above me. The table rattled as she picked something up.

The shears. With a sick feeling in my stomach, I watched as Lady Cavendish walked to the middle of the room, with the sharp tools in her hand.

What was she about to do?

I never got the chance to find out.

With a deafening howl, the creature leaped at Lady Cavendish.

"Stop!" Lady Cavendish cried.

The creature pinned her against the far wall. The shears clattered to the floor.

The creature, raised to its fullest extent, towered over her. The tree on its back shivered, its branches making a creaking sound, like the warning of a rattlesnake's tail. Its webbed feet had claws attached to it, like I'd seen otters in the river by our farm, and it held its long nose up like a sword, as if ready to strike down on Lady Cavendish.

Think, Cora! The plants on the creature's back were fluffed up, like the hackles of a snarling dog. And then I realized. I had seen the fur rise on Maisie, Bill's dog, in just the same way when she was unsure and afraid of something.

The creature was terrified.

By raising her voice, Lady Cavendish had done the worst possible thing. The creature couldn't understand her.

The creature needed someone to speak its language.

I crawled out from under the table.

Herrrooooooooooooooooooooaaaaahhhhhooooo

I called out, making my voice soft.

"Cora!" Lady Cavendish hissed. "What are you doing here? You need to get out, it's not safe."

I ignored her, focusing on the creature, who hadn't backed down from its hind legs, pinning Lady Cavendish to the wall. I called out again, keeping my shoulders relaxed and my palms facing outwards, my arms loose at my side.

"It's all right," I whispered to the frightened animal. "I know you're scared; I would be too, if I was kept in a small room, alone in the dark."

Ever so slowly, the creature's ferns on its back fell flatter. It looked as if it was deflating.

"You can get down now," I said quietly. "You're safe."

The creature dropped to all fours.

I pushed the shears with my foot, sending them skittering under the table.

"There, they can't hurt you now," I whispered. "No one is going to hurt you." I looked at Lady Cavendish pointedly.

Lady Cavendish held her hand to her chest, breathing hard. Her arm was bleeding. She looked from me to the creature then back at me. "I'll leave her alone, for now."

"See?" I spoke to the creature. "No one is going to hurt you."

I was close enough that I could reach out and touch her mossy side. The creature turned her head and watched me, as if daring me to make a move. Slowly, I reached out and gently stroked the moss with my trembling fingers. It was warm and soft.

The tiny flowers tickled my palm.

The creature reached out her long nose and poked my hand with it tentatively. It was as soft as Bella's nose. I brushed the tiny furled ferns that grew out of the moss on her sides, silky as bird feathers. Then the creature curled her trunk around my hand and I forgot how to breathe for a moment.

"Extraordinary," Lady Cavendish whispered, but I hardly noticed her presence any more. The dark and cold room melted away until it was just the creature and me. Like the ferns that unfurled on her back, it felt as though tiny, invisible tendrils were beginning to grow in the space between us, as a connection formed. I gently brushed my hand down her long nose, feeling rough skin under my palm. The creature's eyes fluttered; all of that strain and fear must have tired her out. With a sigh, she knelt down and curled into a ball, like a cat, although she was as big as Bella. She tucked her long nose around her and closed her eyes.

"Come," said Lady Cavendish. Reluctantly, I followed her out of the room.

"Do we have to leave her here?" I asked, as Lady Cavendish shut the door behind us. "It's dark and cold."

"We can talk about this in the morning," Lady Cavendish said.

"Why is she down here?" I insisted. "And *what* is she?"

"We will talk about this in the morning, Cora," Lady Cavendish said again, more firmly.

I followed Lady Cavendish along the underground hallway, then up the stairways until she came to a door in the wall. It opened into Lady Cavendish's room.

"Goodnight, Cora." Lady Cavendish waited pointedly, and I continued my way up the stairs to my room.

Softly, I closed the secret door behind me and turned off the torch. I hid the torch under my pillow and nestled under the covers.

With my eyes tight shut, I saw the strange creature, with a garden on her back.

Chapter 15

Creatures of the Four Realms

The moment my eyes opened, my whole body felt heavy as lead.

I had dreamed of the creature, of plants of every colour. Every time I had surfaced, I had listened for the calls, but I hadn't heard it again.

Was the creature awake now? Was she afraid?

I was determined to find a way to see the creature again. But before that, I had to see Lady Cavendish.

I dressed hurriedly and clattered downstairs, taking the steps two at a time. Out of breath, I knocked on Lady Cavendish's door. "Come in," came the voice.

Lady Cavendish was sitting behind her desk, reading. The grey hair around her ears looked white in the light of the desk lamp that was still on despite the sunshine outside. She peered at me over the top of her glasses. Ornaments were dotted around the desk, wooden sculptures of animals and birds and odd-looking ceramic creations. It was as if Lady Cavendish was just another object in a mountain of things, another item in her own collection.

Lady Cavendish snapped the book shut.

I scanned the cover. *Creatures of the Four Realms.* I longed to see inside it. I also wanted to know about the creature I'd met last night. What was her name? Where did she come from? Would I be allowed to see her again? And more importantly, why was she being hidden away?

But in my excitement, I lost my voice. It got stuck somewhere in my throat, all jammed up and useless. Instead, I gazed at Lady Cavendish expectantly.

Lady Cavendish studied me for a long moment. "You're not very talkative, are you?" There was no accusation in her statement. She said it as if she was observing the behaviour of a bird or other animal.

I went over to the chair and sat down.

"I'm assuming you would like to know about the creature, Cora." Lady Cavendish stood up.

I nodded eagerly. I felt breathless and slightly dizzy.

"My mother and father were explorers," Lady Cavendish said. "They travelled the many realms of the world and brought back extraordinary creatures to Direspire Hall, as well as other artefacts and treasures."

Perhaps, I thought, that explained the paintings and the wooden statues and the boxes and boxes of papers.

"I am the caretaker of their life's work." Lady Cavendish gestured at the cluttered study. "I keep their legacy secure, and that includes the menagerie."

This troubled me. I had never liked the idea that Bella our cow was a belonging, a thing to be milked. She was my friend and part of my family. And these creatures were living, breathing beings that deserved to live happy lives, just like anybody else.

Lady Cavendish put down *Creatures of the Four Realms* on the table in front of me, where it sat just out of reach. I clamped my hands in my pocket.

"This is my parents' book. They were particularly interested in studying and identifying the extraordinary creatures that they found on their travels. Mostly, they are scribbles and smatterings of description; my parents were impatient and impulsive and their attention was easily ensnared and then lost." Lady Cavendish pushed her reading glasses further up the bridge of her nose. "My parents believed that there are four realms in the world, The Clouds, The Seas, The Deep Earth and The Land. The Land is largely inhabited by humans, while the other realms hold many extraordinary creatures. My parents attempted to document the creatures that lived in each one.

"The pangea – which you saw last night – is one such creature. She can grow in response to light and space, which is why I must keep her in the dark. If given light, she will grow at a considerable rate, and she won't stop growing, not while there is space for her to grow. Can you imagine that, Cora? Trying to contain a creature the size of an island, or even a *whole continent*? Right now, she is a manageable size, but she has to be pruned, and we need to cut off any new growth and never let her go into sunlight."

"But that must hurt her, to be pruned, when all she wants to do is grow!" I remembered the shears in Lady Cavendish's hands, and the fright in the creature's eyes. "Isn't there another way?"

"The pangea is precious, Cora. It is said that she is the very key to life itself." Lady Cavendish's eyes took on a faraway look. "My parents risked everything to find the egg and bring it back here. All those years, I kept it safe and hidden. And now, finally, the egg has hatched. I'm not going to risk having her stolen."

Can I see her again? I wanted to ask, but I was afraid of the answer.

"I didn't tell you about her because I didn't think you could handle her. But, after seeing you with her last night, I'm happy for you to take over her feeding and her care. But she must be kept a secret. Is that understood?" Lady Cavendish passed a hand over her eyes. "I've kept the creatures of Direspire Hall alive all these years, including watching over the hatching of the pangea, but it is time for someone else to take on their care. I want more time to paint, and to organize the artefacts and books that my parents left behind. It would be a relief if you could care for the pangea – then I can focus on what's important."

There's nothing more important than the creatures, I wanted to say. *They're alive, while all the clutter and papers and relics in Direspire Hall are just* things.

"You will need to feed the creature seawater," Lady Cavendish grabbed a pen from a chipped ceramic pot and turned her attention to a sheaf of paper. "You can begin by pruning her new shoots this morning, seeing as I wasn't able to manage it yesterday."

My heart sank. After seeing how angry and frightened the creature had been when Lady Cavendish had tried to prune her, that was the last thing I wanted to do. And yet, as creature keeper, I had no choice.

Chapter 16
Pruning the Pangea

Even though it was morning, my torch was the only light travelling down to the underground corridor of the secret passageway. Stepping into the darkness was disorientating; I couldn't imagine what it must be like for the pangea, who knew nothing else.

I knocked softly on the door to her room, to let her know that I was here.

Hearing nothing from inside the room, I cracked the door open and slipped inside.

I fumbled along the table, until I found the lamp and lit it. The room glowed in orange light, and I turned off the torch.

I saw the pangea then. She had backed herself away into the corner of the room, as far away from me as possible. The ferns along her back rose up. She rocked herself from side to side in an agitated manner and hissed at me.

"Do you remember me?" I spoke softly, not wanting to scare her. "I'm Cora, your new keeper." I held my hands out, palm open, to show her that I didn't have anything to hide.

The creature trumpeted, the strange sonorous harrumph that made my ears tingle.

Herrrooooooooooooooooooooaaaaahhhhhooooo

Taking a deep breath, I repeated the call back to her. I couldn't mimic exactly the echoing, eerie sound that made the hairs on my arm stand up, but it seemed to do the trick. The creature stopped rocking. The ferns on her back slowly subsided, with a whispery swish, and the vines uncurled down her sides. Even the flowers opened up, their brightly coloured petals catching the soft glow of the lamp.

I scanned the room. In the corner, the trough was filled with water. There was straw for the creature to sleep on, but nothing much else. I took a step forward and my foot crunched on something.

I stooped and picked up a piece of pale blue

eggshell. Turning it over in my hands, I was surprised at how heavy it was. Lady Cavendish had said that the creature had hatched recently.

"Is this part of your egg?" I asked the creature, placing the shell on the table. "I would have given anything to see you hatch!" What a sight that would have been. "It's a shame you've been stuck inside ever since."

The creature sighed. Trotting round in a small circle, she flumped to the floor, tucking her trunk around her body like a scarf. If it wasn't for her watchful eyes that followed me around the room, she would have looked just like a small hill, with a meadow and a tree on top. Yellow, blue and pink daisies dotted across her flank, as well as tangles of thorny roses and tubular flowers, similar to foxgloves.

It seemed like such a shame, to cut those blooms. And I knew how the creature felt about being pruned. But an order was an order.

I crept over to the table and reached for the shears. The soft glow of the lamplight gleamed off the sharp edges. My fingers had only just gripped the handles, when the creature erupted from her resting place. She jumped to her feet with a deafening howl.

I dropped the shears and pressed my hands over my ears. The noise was so loud that I felt the cobbles shake under my feet. Dust shivered down from the ceiling. The tormented howl would surely have been heard all across the moors. Hastily, I kicked the shears under the table.

The creature stood, panting, eyes wide. I could see myself reflected in them, suddenly seeing myself as she did; someone who was going to hurt her. A monster.

"I'm so sorry," I whispered. "I don't *want* to do it, it's just what I've been told to do."

Maybe the pruning could wait, I thought. The creature wasn't going to let me anywhere near her right now. She huddled in the corner of the room, her feet planted as if ready to charge if I went anywhere near the shears again. Her eyes watched me anxiously.

"Maybe it's best if I come back later," I said. Leaving the creature like this, more frightened than when I'd arrived, felt all wrong. This wasn't what a creature keeper was supposed to do. But I knew that by staying, I was only making it worse. Besides, I had a whole list of other creatures that needed caring for today and I was going to be late. With a heavy heart, I blew out the lamplight and closed the door behind me.

Once out of the room and into the hallway, I noticed a glimmer of light at the furthest end of the passageway, in the opposite direction to the stairs heading to my attic.

Curious, I followed the corridor until I came to a small set of steps leading to a trapdoor. Shoving my back against the door, I lifted it up with a creak and found myself peering out into the sunlit garden, where the early morning mist swirled.

I clambered out on to the grass outside. It was early enough that mist clung in droplets to the blades of grass and dampened my socks, but I barely noticed. Even though I hated how I'd left the creature in the secret room, the thought of seeing the creatures in the glasshouse pulled me through the tangle of briars and bluebells.

As the house disappeared behind the trees, I felt an odd feeling of release, like the house was an unsettling song that you only noticed once it had finished playing.

In the clearing, the glasshouse stood dazzling in the bright sunlight.

Nearby, Griff was digging the weeds out of the geranium bed. He waved to me enthusiastically and I waved back.

He had attempted to make a trellis for the running beans with sticks and cord, but it was leaning heavily to one side, so that the plants couldn't get enough sunlight. He had left ripened tomatoes to rot on the ground, attracting burrowing beetles.

I bent down and plucked some of the salvageable fruit.

"Did you hear something, just now?" I asked him curiously. "A howling?" Although I'd told Lady Cavendish that I wouldn't tell anyone about the creature in the basement, it was hard to imagine that no one else could hear her.

Griff scrunched his nose up. "Yup, Ma and me have both heard it, and Mr Johnson has been going mad trying to find it, but Lady Cavendish says it's the pipes. Old house, old pipes."

"What do you mean, Mr Johnson's been trying to find it?" I hadn't considered the possibility that he wouldn't know about the creature.

"I've seen him, knocking on walls when he thinks I'm not watching. He's looking for something, and it's not pipes."

"Doesn't that all seem strange to you?"

"Of course! I've been driving myself round the bend wanting to find out what's making those noises." Griff shrugged. "But when you're on the run, you don't ask too many questions, otherwise you'll get people asking questions in return."

Startled, I raised my eyebrow. "You never told me that! So you ran away from your pa?" I should have guessed all along.

"See, questions! That's what happens when I get too nosy." Griff sighed, before looking around cautiously. "When Pa's *Marvellous Travelling Menagerie* stopped at Brambury Town a few weeks ago, we escaped. He doesn't know we're here."

Griff's horrible pa. "I'm glad you escaped," I said wholeheartedly.

"Ma said we had to find somewhere that Pa would never think to look for us, a place that had been forgotten about. When Ma saw the walls of Direspire Hall, she said this was the right place for us. We were lucky Lady Cavendish was in the orchard that night and heard us ringing the bell, instead of Mr Johnson. She listened and let us through the gates. We've been here ever since. You won't tell anyone, will you?" Griff's eyes widened.

"Of course, I won't," I reassured him. It was brave of Griff to confide in me about his horrible pa, especially since we'd only just met.

Griff brightened, like the sun appearing behind a storm cloud. "I'm glad you're here. It'll be much less boring!"

"I'm glad you're here too," I said to Griff. And I really was. I was glad he was safe. And I found it easy to talk to him, which was no small thing.

"Well, you don't have to worry about your pa here," I said. "Everyone is too scared to come anywhere near Direspire Hall, and the gate is locked."

"I wish I was a better gardener, though," Griff muttered, nudging a fallen tomato with his boot.

"We can feed the tortoises these, so they won't go to waste," I said to Griff.

At least the lettuce was heathy, with dark green outer leaves. I sliced off a couple of lettuce heads and Griff unfolded a paper bag from his pocket for me to collect the vegetables in.

Griff heaved the paper bag up and together we headed for the glasshouse.

The glasshouse glittered, splintering the early

morning sun. To my surprise, Mr Johnson was there, his hand on the glasshouse door. He was wearing the same navy overcoat that he'd been wearing the night before, and walking boots splattered with mud. Had he been out all night?

When he saw us, his expression darkened. "I'm just making sure you're keeping the glasshouse locked," he said, scowling. "You look like the forgetful type."

And what does the forgetful type look like exactly? I wanted to retort, but the words stuck to my tongue. Griff gave me a look, that included an eye-roll and a twitch of a smile. I bit down on my lip, to stop a snort of laughter from bubbling out.

"I'll be keeping an eye on you both," Mr Johnson snapped, before stomping back towards Direspire Hall.

"He's in a good mood," Griff muttered. I unlocked the heavy lock and pushed open the door.

To my delight, the tortoises seemed to be waiting for us, right near the entrance. One of them craned their long neck towards me.

I scooted down and held out a lettuce leaf. The tortoise moved towards me, surprisingly fast, and nibbled at the leafy green.

Griff shivered.

"Imagine it snapping your finger," he said, tucking his hands in his armpits.

Leaving the tortoise with the tomatoes and the rest of the lettuce, I peeked into the moonbird enclosure. The birds were slumbering, their beaks tucked under their wings. It was time to begin my tasks.

Working with Griff, I scattered birdseed for Echo, tossed shrimp into the pond where the perch swam and changed the water in the pangolin's bowl. Taking out my notebook, I checked off the list of instructions from Lady Cavendish one by one. Check, check, check. With every tick off the list, I felt my confidence grow.

Griff appeared with a large fish from the cold storage. "I've got the seacat's breakfast!"

When we arrived at the seacat's enclosure, we found someone already there.

"Mr Johnson," I said. "You're here again. Can I help you with anything?"

Mr Johnson turned and scrutinized us for an uncomfortable moment, his frown deepening.

I gritted my teeth and held his stare, while Griff shifted uneasily next to me. Mr Johnson had the sort of glare that made you doubt yourself and wrack your brains for something you must have done wrong. My throat clamped up in the familiar way, closing around my voice like a brick wall.

Mr Johnson mouth twisted unpleasantly. "As I said, I wanted to check you're keeping on top of things."

I peered into the enclosure. All I could see of the blue-and-black striped cat was its emerald eyes, just above the clean pond. *We were the ones who cleaned out the enclosure, in case you hadn't noticed,* I thought angrily. I watched Mr Johnson swat away a butterfly, sending it spinning into a rose bush, where it became trapped in the thorns.

Mr Johnson marched off back towards the entrance of the glasshouse, his boots pounding on the brick path. I watched as he stopped to wipe a splatter of mud off them, muttering under his breath, before stomping out of sight.

Once he had disappeared, I went to the rose bush and freed the trapped butterfly. Thankfully, its delicate blue wings were unharmed and after a pause, it fluttered up into the air to join the others.

"He's a rotten egg." Griff jutted out his chin. "Always snooping around, looking for an excuse to shout at someone. When we first came here, Ma and me, he didn't like that one bit. He wanted Lady Cavendish to turn us away at the gates. Said we had an *ulterior motive*." Griff screwed up his nose. "Ma says that means he didn't believe us when we said we needed help, which I don't understand. Why would we come here if we were fine? I'd much rather be living in the town, making new friends, rather than pretending to be a gardener in this old place."

That last bit made me feel strange. Was Griff only my friend because there was no one else? The air in the glasshouse suddenly felt too stuffy. This was the problem with being friends with people instead of animals.

"Let's go and feed the glass dragon," I said, setting quickly off down the path, with Griff hurrying after me. I wasn't here to make friends. I was here to do a good job as creature keeper.

Chapter 17

Feeding the Dragon

The glass dragon swooped through the mist in its large enclosure. It was easier to spot now that I'd become accustomed to its shape. It was like looking at a window; you knew it was there, even if you couldn't always *see* the glass.

"Is it in there?" said Griff nervously.

"Yes, she's there. You don't need to worry," I said. I could understand why Griff was frightened of creatures. If his pa had regularly threatened to have him eaten, anyone would be the same. I wished he would give the seacat and the glass dragon a chance, though.

Griff peered into the top of the stove. "There are no more leaves in the furnace. We'll have to go and get some more."

I glanced into the open mouth of the furnace. There were only dying embers.

We couldn't just get ordinary leaves, Lady Cavendish had said; we needed the leaves from the whistling trees. A shiver of excitement went through me. I was going to see the strange, tall trees up close for the first time!

"The thing is," Griff grimaced. "Mr Johnson has the key to the gated garden, where the trees are. We'll have to ask him to let us in."

Back inside Direspire Hall, we went looking for Mr Johnson.

"Why does Mr Johnson have the keys to the gated garden? You're the gardener," I said to Griff. "Surely you should be able to go where you like in the grounds of Direspire Hall."

"He said I would only go and lose them," Griff said.

As we navigated through the cluttered hallway, I almost tripped over a glass terrarium on the floor. Inside, there were tiny ferns, growing among a collection of rocks.

The ferns in the terrarium reminded me of the creature, the pangea, and I felt a jolt of sorrow for her, stuck in her dark room. As soon as I had an opportunity to head back down to see her, I would.

I opened a door on the left of the main entrance, which must have been the dining room, although it hadn't been used in years by the looks of it.

"We're not supposed to go in there!" Griff said, following me inside.

In the middle of the room there was a table that could easily fit twenty or so people around it, with an ornate chandelier hanging above it. There was a huge fireplace filled with ash. Cobwebs dripped from the chandelier and dust covered the table like a cloth. The curtains hung off their railings as if they'd given up trying to hide the disarray from the outside world. In a glass case, a single white vase covered in delicate blue paintwork stood on display.

A strange itch tickled the back of my throat. All of this dust and disorder, in a room that should have been full of people and chatter and warmth.

There were so many *things*. Velvet boxes with their mouths snapped open displayed jewels that soaked up the glow from the bulb, splintering the soft light. Amber, blue, green and black glass bottles lined up on one of the cabinet shelves, some with raised lettering, of which I could only read: *Do Not...*

There was a collection of stuffed squirrels, all sitting at a small table, as if having a meal together. Their eyes were tiny black beads, sewn on with none of Ma's neatness, so that they looked extremely surprised to find themselves in such a strange predicament. I stroked one of the squirrels gently on the head with the tip of my finger.

On the wall, there were framed paintings of butterflies, so life-like it seemed they could flutter away on a breath. Huge blue and red specimens, others with yellow spotted wings with dots like eyes, nothing like I'd ever seen before. It was only when I got closer that I realized they weren't paintings at all, but *real* butterflies pressed between two panes of glass.

"How cruel!" I said. "This room is so strange."

"I bet there were brilliant parties in here once." Griff peeked into a cardboard box that had mildew growing on its sides. He reached in and pulled out a sheaf of photos, black-and-white ones.

"Look at this one!" Griff handed one to me and the others fell out of his hands like a pack of cards, spilling on the floor. While he scrambled to pick them up, I studied the photo.

It was of Direspire Hall. Even though it was black and white, I could *feel* the colour. Roses lined the path and the dense ivy covered the front of the building. My eyes filled the scene with green and red and pink.

There were three figures in the photo. The day it had been taken must have been sunny; they were all shading their eyes or squinting against the bright light.

A woman and a man wearing loose-fitting shirts and trousers, much like Lady Cavendish wore, both with dark hair and dark eyes. They stood on the steps, their arms around each other. The woman was laughing at the man, who looked very pleased with himself. They both looked happy.

Lower down on the photo, on the very last step before the ground, sat a small child.

She was gazing up at the man and the woman, as if afraid they were about to disappear, or like she couldn't quite believe they were really there. Her face was thin and pale and she was pressing her lips together in a frown.

"Who do you think they are?" Griff cleared a space on the table with his forearm and deposited the rest of the photos. "Could it be Lady Cavendish and her ma and pa?"

"It must be," I said. She had the same stormy look on her face, even then. The clever eyes of a crow. They were the same eyes that gazed out of Lady Cavendish's paintings in her study. It seemed strange to me, why anyone would paint people who were no longer there, over and over again. Lady Cavendish could paint the pangea, with her beautiful garden, with colourful flowers and delicate ferns, or the seacat's emerald eyes.

"There are more photos, look." Griff fanned the photos out. There were photos of birds and animals and mountains and forests. Some were taken at sea – the prow of a boat crashing through waves, or a slice of a sail against the sky.

Sometimes it was just the man in a photo, sometimes the woman, and sometimes they were pictured together, paddling in the sea or stalking through a forest of leafy trees with strange sausage-shaped fruit.

I looked for another image of the small girl, but apart from the one photo taken on the steps of Direspire Hall, there were none.

I wondered whether Lady Cavendish had ever

longed for adventure, like I did. Her parents had travelled the world and she had been left behind, at Direspire Hall.

"I wish I could go to amazing places like this." Griff jabbed his finger at one picture. "Look, that one is taken from the top of a mountain. You can see the clouds *below* them!"

It did look magical. A world above the clouds. Could this be where the moonbirds and the glass dragon came from? Thinking of the glass dragon, I was reminded why we were here.

"Come on," I said to Griff. "We'd better keep looking for Mr Johnson."

We found Mr Johnson in the library, sitting at a small, velvet-covered table. He was engrossed in a book, *How to Transport Extraordinary Creatures,* and there was a pile of other books next to him.

The huge room smelled musty. It was full to the brim with curiosities and shelves of books that stretched far above, all the way up to the ceiling.

There were so many things that snagged my attention, tugging my eyes from one object to the next. There was a globe, with islands painted on its surface, surrounded by a sea that had faded to dusty blue. Sea monsters with bulging eyes and needle-spiked spines were dotted amid the blue. My hands itched to spin the globe on its axis.

Animals carved out of wood lined a low shelf, some with long necks that stretched longer that their bodies and some with fangs carved out of bone. I reached out to touch one of them.

Mr Johnson snapped the book shut, making me jump. "And why are you two skulking around, eh?"

Griff spoke up. "We need the key to the gated garden. We're going to gather leaves for the glass dragon's furnace."

I picked up a book from the pile on the table and blew the dust off the cover. *The Secrets in the Skies*, by Lord and Lady Cavendish.

"Give me that." Mr Johnson reached over and snatched the book from my hands. "That's not yours."

It's not yours either, I wanted to say. All the books on the table had exciting titles, like, *The Hollow Worms of the Deep Earth* and *The Sky Jellyfish: Myth or Reality?*

Mr Johnson unhooked a silver key from his belt.

"Give the key back when you're done. And no more skulking around. Direspire Hall is not a playground."

The insult stung. I wasn't just a child. I was the creature keeper, and I was only trying to do my job.

Chapter 18

The Whistling Trees

"Welcome to the gated garden," Griff said ceremoniously.

We stood in front of the wrought iron gates, which were orange with rust and had vicious-looking spikes along the top. Through the gates, I could make out the silvery trunks of the misty trees, shimmering like the wings of the moonbirds. Griff had brought a wheelbarrow with him.

He jiggled the key in the lock and with a *clank* it turned.

Once inside, we crossed a patch of boggy grass that smelled of the moors, of heather and peat. It smelled of home, and for a moment I missed the farm, with Bella and Ma and Pa and Crabbit. On the edge of the patch of grass, the whistling trees stood, surrounded by a white fog that billowed upwards, like bonfire smoke, before joining the clouds that hung over this part of the Direspire grounds.

"The leaves of the whistling tree smoulder once they fall from the branches," Griff said, echoing what Lady Cavendish had told me. He stopped on the edge of the fog. "You'll see what I mean."

Pushing the wheelbarrow, he trundled into the hazy woods. Following in his footsteps, I almost expected to feel a chill across my bare arms, like an early morning mist, but the fog was warm, and smelled sweet, and slightly nutty.

I looked down to see that, littering the ground, the fallen leaves were smouldering around their edges, sending plumes of sweet-smelling smoke upwards.

Overhead, the drum of a woodpecker ricocheted and, here, protected from the winds by the tall trees, I thought I could just about hear the faint bleat of the sheep, grazing on the moors.

Hidden behind the walls of Direspire Hall, it was easy to forget that there was a whole world outside, where Ma and Pa still lived. The thought of them carrying on with their days without me was strange, and although there was comfort in the fact that everything was the same out there, it made me feel sad for a moment. I didn't think adventure would feel like this: excitement for the unknown and a longing for home, a battle between them both.

Further into the forest we went, collecting the silvery fallen leaves from the whistling trees and putting them into the barrow. The leaves were shaped like an arrowhead and almost as sharp.

I yelped as the edge of a leaf sliced through the bit of skin between my thumb and forefinger. Blood bloomed in the cut.

"You could have warned me," I muttered to Griff, sucking my thumb.

Griff pulled a handkerchief from his pocket. "It's clean, I promise!" he said, handing it to me. "Put pressure on the cut, it will stop bleeding after a bit. I've had to collect the leaves lots of times, with Lady Cavendish."

I pressed the cloth to the cut. "I know what to do. I've fixed enough bandages," I said, thinking of Bella's infected hoof and Wildling's wounds from Crabbit's sharp teeth.

"I was only trying to help," Griff said. "You don't

always need to know *everything*."

I was just about to tell Griff that he was wrong, that there were lots of things I didn't know, when an eerie shriek made me jump. As the scream built, the leaves stirred, swirling into the air like a swarm of silver butterflies. I was glad I was wearing long socks, or my ankles would have been cut to shreds. I pressed my hands over my ears as the shriek reached a crescendo, then petered out in a low moan.

"What was that?" I gasped, peering up at the canopy of leaves.

"It's the trees. They whistle in the wind, that's what gives them the name. It made me jump too, the first time I heard it." Griff scooped up another handful of leaves, keeping his fingers carefully tucked into the long sleeves of his coat. The barrow was full to the top now. "We're done here; we can head back to the glasshouse."

But staring up at the canopy had given me an idea. Stepping up to the nearest tree, I caught hold of the lowest branch, and hoisted myself up.

"What are you doing, Cora?" Griff hissed.

"What does it look like?" I said. "I'm climbing the tree!" The trunk was slippery smooth, but there were enough boughs to lever myself up.

"Why? We've got enough leaves for the glass dragon."

I peered down at Griff's pale face, scrunched up with concern.

"I'll just be a minute," I said. "I want to see if I can spot my farm from up here; I should be able to see over the wall!"

Being careful to avoid the razor-sharp leaves, I pulled myself up another branch. A gust of muggy wind shook the branch and caused another unearthly shriek from the trees. I risked a look around. A little bit further and I would soon be able to see over the wall.

As I reached for the next branch though, my hands fumbled to find purchase on the smooth bark. My foot slipped and I found myself unbalanced, nothing but thin air under my swinging leg. I grabbed hold of the trunk, sending a shower of sharp leaves raining down. I pressed my face against the trunk and I caught my breath.

"Are you OK?" Griff called, sounding distant.

Peering around, I could just about see the top of the wall, but the mist from the smouldering leaves below obscured the view.

I looked up. I still couldn't see the top of the trees. They disappeared into the misty haze.

If I climbed any higher, I would disappear too. It was a tantalizing thought, that there was nothing, or *everything*, just beyond reach. A world above the clouds, just like in the photograph we'd seen.

The wind gusted through the leaves again. All I could hear now was the whistling-shriek of the trees all around me, so shrill that my ears ached. I felt suddenly dizzy. I needed to be back on solid ground, and I wasn't going to see the farm through the cloud anyway.

As quickly as I could, I retraced the path down the tree, being careful not to put a foot wrong this time.

It was only when I stumbled to the ground that I felt my heartbeat slow back to normal.

"You look like you've seen a ghost!" Griff helped me up. "Did you see your farm?"

I shook my head, unable to speak. My ears still rang with the whistling trees.

"Come on," said Griff. "Let's get back to work."

A voice called out to us.

"You've taken your time."

It was Mr Johnson. I groaned. He seemed to be

any place that we were today.

"We've finished collecting the leaves," Griff said, leaving out the part where I'd climbed one of the trees. "We're leaving now."

"The geraniums need cutting back, near the fountain," Mr Johnson said. "I'll be having words with Lady Cavendish if you don't keep on top of the gardening."

"Yes, Mr Johnson," Griff replied, kicking out at a tuft of grass growing between the bricks on the path. I felt as crestfallen as Griff looked; I'd hoped that he could stay helping me all day.

Mr Johnson turned on his heel and left. I locked the gated garden and realized I needed to give the keys back to him. I thought about running after him – but then I changed my mind. I didn't want to have to ask Mr Johnson for the keys every time we had to feed the glass dragon – the less I had to interact with him, the better. Maybe he'd forget that I had them. I slipped the keys into my pocket.

Back at the glass dragon's enclosure, we shovelled the smouldering silvery leaves in the steam machine, keeping the coals burning.

The glass dragon appeared to enjoy the stoked-up furnace and swirled in the fog.

Her haunting call, that shivered through the air, reminded me of the sound that the wind made, through the boughs of snow-covered trees. She seemed so delicate, as if she could shatter at any moment. It made me want to protect her at all costs.

"I'm going to call her Brittle," I decided.

"You're good at names," Griff said approvingly. "I wonder why Lady Cavendish hasn't named them before?"

I wondered that too.

While Griff spent the afternoon gardening, I attended to the creatures. It was while I was collecting fallen apples for Echo the macaw that I heard the entrance bell to Direspire Hall ringing.

Before I could move, Mr Johnson hurried past, looking agitated.

"I'll deal with it, Cora," he barked, heading down the drive. "Make yourself useful."

I carried on collecting the apples, ignoring him. Why was he in such a hurry to get to the gate before me? Then I remembered seeing him sneak out of the house last night. Was he up to something?

I knew it was silly to get on the wrong side of someone as horrible as Mr Johnson, but I let my curiosity lead the way. I kept myself hidden around the side of Direspire Hall, staying in the cover of the shrubbery until I could see Mr Johnson.

As I watched, he glanced up at the windows of Direspire Hall. There was something furtive about it. He didn't want to be seen.

As the gate came into view, I ducked into the woods, behind the large oak trees, my feet in the bluebells. I was close enough to peep out, but try as I might, I couldn't catch sight of who was behind the gate.

Mr Johnson reached the gate. He was breathing hard. "I told you not to ring the bell. You can't just waltz in here. She'll never allow it."

"I thought you ran the place? That's the impression you gave last night," a deep voice answered, with a fair amount of scorn. "I've come to collect what I paid for."

"It's too soon. There's still a missing piece to the puzzle. I need more time."

"I don't like games, Arthur," the voice commanded. "If I get a sniff of trickery, you won't see another penny. Is that understood?"

Mr Johnson nodded, before turning around and trotting back to Direspire Hall, with the air of a dog that had just been told off. If he'd had a tail, it would have been tucked between his legs. Whatever had just happened between Mr Johnson and the stranger at the gate, I decided to tell Lady Cavendish. She needed to know if Mr Johnson was up to something – because whatever it was, it didn't sound good.

Chapter 19

Gathering Moonlight

I knocked on Lady Cavendish's study door and, when I heard her call, let myself in.

Lady Cavendish sat on the floor, a large sketchbook open in front of her. She was engrossed in sketching out a portrait of someone who looked just like her. Dark eyes, and a smile that hovered between sad and joyful, as if not knowing quite which to feel.

I recognized the woman from the photo. It was the one Griff and I had guessed must be Lady Cavendish's ma.

"That's beautiful," I said. I could never draw like that.

"Do you ever fear that you will lose a person all over again, by forgetting how their eyes used to shine?" Lady Cavendish swept the pencil down the paper, sketching a curl along a cheek. "It's a grief that never really leaves you."

Lady Cavendish suddenly looked much smaller among the cluttering of things in her room and her eyes were sad. I knew what it was like to feel lonely.

"Maybe you could draw something else instead?" I suggested, hoping I was saying the right words. "The pangea has some beautiful flowers. You could draw her?"

Lady Cavendish closed the sketchbook with a snap and smiled faintly.

"What can I do for you, Cora?"

My tongue twisted into a knot. But I couldn't let this go unsaid.

"It's Mr Johnson." I faltered. "There was a stranger at the gate. He – I think it was a man – was asking Mr Johnson about a . . . puzzle. I thought you should know."

To my surprise, Lady Cavendish laughed. "My parents' discoveries and explorations of the natural world are well known, Cora." She paused, then said, "There's always someone coming to the gates – scientists and collectors and those who are curious about the creatures themselves, the seacat and the glass dragon and so forth, or those with morbid curiosity who'd heard about the accident all those years ago. Mr Johnson knows to send them on their way."

"But..." I began, and Lady Cavendish shot me a look.

"I won't hear any slander about Arthur," she said sharply. "I know he can be a difficult man, but he has looked after Direspire Hall since I was very young. I trust him implicitly."

I nodded, swallowing down my protest. If Lady Cavendish said Mr Johnson could be trusted, who was I to say otherwise? But I couldn't ignore the sense of prickling unease, like a persistent nettle rash. No matter what Lady Cavendish said, something wasn't right about what I'd seen.

"There's a full moon tonight," Lady Cavendish said, changing the subject. "You can gather moonlight for the moonbirds."

"Yes, Lady Cavendish," I muttered. My eyes caught on the cover of a book that Lady Cavendish had left on the side of the dresser. *Creatures of the Four Realms.*

I glanced at Lady Cavendish; she had opened her sketchbook and was drawing again. I shot out my hand and grabbed the book, tucking it under my jumper, next to my hammering heart.

Quick as a mouse, I left the room and scampered up to the attic.

What was I thinking? Why did I take the book? I pulled it out from under my jumper and stared at it. It would help me learn more about the creatures, especially the mysterious pangea. *I'll only borrow it,* I thought to myself. Carefully, I tucked it under my pillow to look at later.

The dew was settling on the grass in frosty patches as Griff and I walked through the orchard. Overhead, a barn owl glided from one gnarled apple tree to another and bats thrummed through the air on leathery wings. I was glad to see the moon was full with no clouds. I imagined it would make the strange process of catching moonlight for the birds easier.

I shone my torch to light our path.

"Everything smells different at night," Griff whispered, snuffling his nose in the air.

"You don't need to whisper, Griff!" I laughed, although I understood why he was, and my voice wasn't much louder. There was something about being out after sunset that brought the quiet out of you. I was glad that Griff had wanted to join in the night feeding.

I flicked the torch at a flash of movement and caught the white-tipped tail of a fox in the beam.

The glasshouse appeared like a big sugar cube as we rounded the corner of Direspire Hall. The panes reflected the moonlight differently, a softer glow than harsh sunlight.

Inside, the humid air wasn't quite as stuffy as it was during the day. It was cooler too and I was glad I'd worn my jacket.

"Let's gather the moonlight first," I said to Griff. From the store room, I pulled down the copper bowl from the nail it was hanging on. It was surprisingly light for its size and easy to carry with two handles on either side of the round edge. I carried it over my head like an umbrella.

From the pond in the middle of the glasshouse, we filled the copper bowl with water. I picked out a few strands of waterweed and pebbles from the bottom so that it was clear.

"What now?" Griff poked his reflection in the bowl of water, sending ripples across the surface. "It just looks like water to me."

"Lady Cavendish told me to take it outside, so

that we can see the reflection of the moon on the water."

We carried the bowl between us, heavy with pond water. Trying to keep in step with Griff was like trying to predict which way a flea was going to leap. The water sloshed down my trousers and into my boots, leaving a dark trail behind us on the path.

Once outside, we set the bowl on the grass.

"Now what?" Griff bounced up and down with excitement. I shooed him away from the bowl, so that both our shadows were out of the way.

"Let's just see what happens." I studied the bowl from a distance.

The moon shone brightly down on us. The light glittered on the ripples that we'd made by plonking the bowl down, but it still just looked like a bowl of water to me.

We stood like that for a while, watching the moonlight dance along the ripples, until the water became still and we could see the face of the moon, like a ball of goat's cheese on a round plate.

I consulted my notebook. "Lady Cavendish says to swirl the water," I said. "Clockwise. What can we use to stir the water?"

Griff hurried over to the nearby flower bed.

"Maybe one of these stakes," he called.

"Sounds good," I said.

Griff came back with a wooden stake that had been supporting the growing plants. "It's a bit muddy."

I wiped most of the mud off the stick on my trouser leg. Then I squatted down and, with both hands, swished the stick in the pot, swirling it clockwise, creating a whirlpool in the middle.

"How long do you have to do it for?" Griff squatted down next to me and peered into the bowl.

"Lady Cavendish had said there needed to be moonlight in the bowl as I spun the water. You're blocking the moonlight!" I scolded Griff.

"Sorry." He rolled back on his haunches.

My arms started to ache. After what seemed to be ages, I felt a change in the water. It began to feel oddly lumpy.

"Look!" Griff peered into the copper bowl and gaped. "It looks like there's cheese in the bowl."

He was right. Small silvery chunks were collecting in the swirls of the water, until they formed a ball.

I stared up at the sky. To my relief, the real moon

was still there, where it should be.

What was in the bowl seemed to be a solid clump of moonlight, like buttermilk churned into butter. "We've done it!" I whooped and me and Griff danced around the bowl, feeling like witches around a cauldron. There was magic in the air. I could feel it.

I'd always dreamed that there was more to life than farming and now I was churning moonlight in a copper bowl.

Careful not to spill a drop, we carried the bowl back into the glasshouse. Now, to feed the birds.

"There's only one pair of ear guards." Griff handed them to me. "Will you be all right by yourself?"

"Of course," I replied, even though I was trembling with nerves. "You stand way back."

Griff walked a way down the path and clamped his hands over his ears. He waved at me with his elbow from a distance.

I snapped the ear guards on to my head and the world descended into a muffled silence.

With one hand around the bowl of moonlight, I unlocked the door to the birdcage and pushed it open. It was heavy, but I managed to open it a fraction, enough to slide inside.

It was hotter in here, humid and sticky. The smell of droppings, both fresh and old, filled my nostrils.

The floor of the enclosure was littered with dead leaves from the branches that had been stacked up for perches. I would need to clean it out as soon as possible. But first, the moonbirds needed feeding.

The white birds had all flown to the other side of the enclosure when I entered. Their feathered chests heaved and their silver wings quivered. All their eyes were on me, tiny beads of fear. Their beaks were wide open, cawing silently.

I placed the bowl carefully on the floor then slowly made my way back to the door and let myself out. I knew that by staying inside, I'd only cause them more distress.

As soon as I was out, I took off the ear guards. Griff bounded over. "Did it work?"

We pressed our faces against the observation window and peered inside.

The moonbirds fluttered towards the bowl on the ground. They eyed the bowl. Then, one brave bird swooped down and perched on the copper rim.

It pecked at the silver ball of moonlight, tearing off a wormlike slither and gulping it down.

This seemed to be all the encouragement the other birds needed. They flocked to the bowl and tore into the moon ball, flittering and shoving and bickering over the pieces, tearing it to shreds until there was nothing left but silver scraps and white feathers floating on the surface of the water.

"The birds look much happier!" Griff pressed his nose against the glass.

"And look, they're shining!" I exclaimed in wonder. The birds were glimmering, as if they were made of starlight. The birdcage glowed a ghostly slivery blue. It was an eerily beautiful, spellbinding sight.

As I stared, a sense of calm came over me. I would have stayed for longer, except there was another extraordinary creature that needed feeding.

"Let's see if the pangolin is out of its burrow," I said to Griff.

From the store room, we gathered a bucket of grubs.

Holding the bucket of grubs close to my chest so that it wouldn't rattle, I sneaked towards the pangolin enclosure.

We crouched next to the wall and I listened

carefully, but the squirmy rustle from hundreds of grubs in the bucket dampened any sounds from the enclosure.

I peeked over the top of the wall. In the silvery light from the moon through the glass ceiling, I caught a glimpse of a scaly tail, before it disappeared down the burrow hole.

"You don't need to hide," I told the shy creature. "I'm here to feed you tasty grubs!" I swung my legs over the low wall and shook out the grubs on the floor of the enclosure. They squirmed over each other in a pile, before inching their way across the sand, leaving squiggly trails behind them.

Stepping back over the wall, I ducked down, but hovered so that I could just see inside. Imagining that I was back in my wildflower meadow at home and letting myself blend into the background, I waited. And waited.

Griff wandered off, whistling his tune through the paths. I heard him throwing pebbles in the waterfall pond. I waited.

And then, out of the burrow came a tiny mouse-like nose. It quivered for a moment, snuffling the air. I held my breath.

The tiny nose became a narrow snout and face,

with bright beady eyes. It must have caught the scent of the juicy grubs, because it trotted out of its burrow into the enclosure.

As small as a cat, overlapping scales covered the creature, from her head to her long, flat tail. She shuffled up to a fat white grub and grabbed it with front claws, then sat on her back legs to eat it in mousy nibbles.

Without realizing, I'd leaned closer to get a better view and the pangolin had spotted me. In an instant, she had curled up into a ball with her long tail wrapped around her body, just like a hedgehog, her overlapping scales acting like a coat of armour.

"Oh, don't be afraid!" I whispered, my heart aching for the scared and scaly creature. "I'm not going to hurt you."

I knew that with a creature as wild as this, the best thing to do was leave them alone as much as possible, like Wildling crow and the badgers I'd observed on the moors. But now I had seen the pangolin and fallen in love with the sweet mouse nose and the endearing way it had tottered towards the grubs.

"I'll call you Pinecone," I said, then I picked up the empty grub bucket and left her in peace.

I felt an enormous sense of happiness and relief.

I'd met all the creatures. And soon I would get to know them all better.

Griff bounced up to me. "Shall we head back?" he said. "This place gives me the creeps at night. You never know what might be lurking around the corner."

"Speaking of lurkers," I said. "There was someone, a man, I think, at the gates earlier. Talking to Mr Johnson."

"What did he look like?" Griff spoke sharply.

"I couldn't see from where I was hiding, and they didn't talk for long. He mentioned speaking to Mr Johnson the night before, something about payment. What do you think Mr Johnson is up to, sneaking out of Direspire at night?"

"Up to no good, whatever it is." Griff bounced nervously, glancing at the shadows between the cherry trees, where Echo roosted in the branches. "I'm surprised Lady Cavendish has put up with him for all these years."

"She didn't have much choice, I suppose." With no one else wanting to work here, Mr Johnson had been mostly in charge. That might also explain why he was so grumpy towards Griff and me all the time: Direspire was no longer under his complete control.

Griff broke through my thoughts. "Race you back to the house!"

Over the tangled roots and bluebells we ran from the darkening shadows of the forest. The sulking shape of Direspire Hall greeted us with a snarl.

Then, out of nowhere it seemed, I bumped straight into someone and we both stumbled backwards. It was Mr Johnson.

"You," Mr Johnson said sharply. "Why are you running around at this hour of the night?"

Why are you *out at night?* I thought, but I kept my mouth shut. Mr Johnson didn't look like he was in any mood to argue.

Griff came to a stop next to me. "We were feeding the moonbirds and the pangolin, sir."

"Well, it's late." He snapped his fingers at us. "Head back inside, before I lock the doors."

Mr Johnson shooed us into Direspire Hall, his lips pressed in a sour line. I glanced at Griff, who wrinkled his nose at me, the disquiet clear in his eyes.

We would have to keep a close eye on the butler from now on, I decided.

Chapter 20
Reading the Book

Once upstairs in my attic room, I pulled the book out from under the pillow.

Although I felt terrible for taking it without permission, the hunger to find out more about the creatures was insufferable. Plus, I would return the book as soon as I'd read it. Lady Cavendish wouldn't even find out, I was sure of it.

Reverently, I reached out and took hold of the heavy book. It was leather-bound and the title *Creatures of the Four Realms* was embossed in silver foil that glinted in the lamplight, as if hinting at the secrets inside.

The spine cracked as I opened it up on my lap.

On the first page, it read:

To our daughter Maggie, who we hope will continue our work.

This notebook is an accumulation of our research trips, where we have attempted to document the many extraordinary creatures of the world. There is nothing more valuable than the natural world, and to gain an appreciation of it, one must see it for oneself. As well as bringing extraordinary creatures back to Direspire Hall with us, we have studied and illustrated those that we found, here in this book.

I read further:

There are many layers to the world, each layer being home to many extraordinary creatures. The creatures that live in the Deep Earth exist in the hollow spaces of the crust, in the cracks and caverns. The Creatures of The Sea never need to touch land. They thrive amid the windstorms and the squalls, where no ship can go. The creatures of the Land are mostly domesticated and tamed, yet a few still remain a mystery.

As I read, my heart beat faster. I was going to catch a glimpse of worlds beyond the moors, even if it was only within the pages of a book.

The creatures of The Clouds. These extraordinary creatures exist above the clouds, out of reach. Birds that drink moonlight and other creatures that have adapted to the sky realm.

The moonbirds!

I read the entire first chapter: "Creatures of the Deep Earth". I found myself gripping the book tightly as I scanned down the page in the torchlight.

There were drawings of creatures I'd never seen or even imagined. Each creature was drawn in ink and painted with soft watercolours, the pale pinks and blues and greys giving each one an eerie pallor. Lizards with too many legs and mouse-like tails. Pale blue snakes in never-ending coils. The way that the artist, either Lord or Lady Cavendish, had painted some of the creatures suggested that they were translucent; the dark rocks could be seen through their sinewy bodies. Roach-like creatures appeared to scuttle across the page, their legs like spiders and pinchers near their mouths.

I read names like *fossil-feeder*, *crust-cruncher* and *hollow-worm*, with descriptions of their various behaviours. I shuddered at the *crust-cruncher*, who ate away at the bedrock with its many sharp teeth. The *fossil-feeder* appeared to be half-spider and half-crab, with an armoured body and snapping jaws attached to eight elongated legs. The description next to it read: *Although rare, the fossil-feeder is highly dangerous. It has been known to snatch unsuspecting prey from above ground, sedating it and dragging it back down to the Deep Earth to devour at its leisure.*

It was fascinating and horrifying at the same time. I'd never imagined creatures like that existing, right under our feet.

There was a world of adventure out there, far from the farms. A world where there were wild things that couldn't be tamed.

The next chapter was called "Creatures of the Sea".

Eagerly, I scanned over the illustrations. Tentacled beings with bulging eyes settled on the seabed among the swaying seaweed. Giant fish lurked on the page. Names like *dragon-squid*, *gulper-eels*, and *scuttle-shark* all jumped out at me. I turned the page, and spotted a familiar creature, with blue and black stripes. It was the spitting image of Tempest, the seacat. In the carefully inked drawing, the seacat dived down, beneath the tumbling waves, using its webbed feet and flat tail, in pursuit of a large fish.

Within each claw, there is fast-acting venom, so that when the seacat swipes its prey, the venom paralyses it, for easier capture.

I thought of Tempest, wallowing in his shallow pool, with no space to dive and hunt for fish. I would talk to Lady Cavendish about him tomorrow, I decided; perhaps we could make the enclosure bigger.

And then I came across a creature with an elephant's trunk and ears, with a garden on its back. It had webbed feet and looked exactly like the creature that I'd seen in the underground room.

The pangea.

Once hatched, the pangea will begin growing vegetation, starting with a sapling, right on the centre of its back, read the description.

There was another illustration of the same creature, only this time, it was huge and floating in water. There was a forest on its back, with a river and a lake. A long nose curled out of the sea like a periscope. Waves crested against its long tusks, frothing into foam and swirling into eddies, where smaller sea creatures surfaced and played in the wakes, creatures that looked like dolphins and seals. The artist had painted birds of every colour and size, swooping among the trees or gliding above the forest. I could make out other animals as well, long-armed creatures swinging from branches and boar-like creatures scurrying between the trees.

It wasn't just a garden that this creature carried on its back, but an entire island.

This extraordinary creature is rarer than any other, with only one born every few thousand years. Unlike the male of the species, who roam the oceans as rocky outcrops, the females grow flora on their backs, and will flourish or wither according to their surroundings. In darkness, the creature will remain undeveloped, but given the right conditions, fresh air and sunlight, the creature will grow rapidly, until it becomes an island, where it will eventually sustain an entire ecosystem of unique flora and fauna.

However, these illustrations are purely theoretical. As we have never seen a pangea in the flesh, we are

basing these designs on legends and myths. We have,
however, managed to find a single egg. It is our hope
that our daughter will raise the pangea from an egg and
complete this book – and our life's work.

The rest of the book was blank pages.

Hiding *Creatures of the Four Realms* under my pillow, I thought about the pangea. She had come all that way, from the sea, only to hatch in a small, dark room underground. She must feel lonely.

I decided that tonight, I would visit her again.

Chapter 21
The Living Island

By this time, the house had settled. It was late.

I pressed my ear to the walls.

Through the wood panelling, I could hear a flutter of sound, the now-familiar groan.

After a moment of searching, I found the secret door latch and the door in the wall swung open. I ducked into the coffin-like passageway.

I crept past the door to Lady Cavendish's room. Her light was still on and I could hear the sound of her moving around, the clink of glass and the swish of water, and her gentle muttering to herself. She must be painting. How many more of those portraits could the walls of Direspire Hall hold? The light from Lady Cavendish's room seeped away as I went down to the underground passageway that was as dark as before. I swept the torch over the walls, training it on the door I knew the pangea was hidden behind.

I opened the door and gave a welcoming "herrroooooooooooaaaaahhhhhooooo", before sitting down on the floor, with enough space between us. After that morning, I wanted to let her know that I was a friend, she didn't have to feel threatened by me.

I marvelled at the dark green moss that bloomed in the crags of her grey skin, with a freckling of tiny yellow flowers. The tree that stood proudly on her back had hand-shaped red leaves and the trunk was supple, swaying with the creature's breathing. A meadow of wildflowers rolled across her shoulders, with delicate blue and red and white blossoms.

I let her watch me and I waited. The silence became comfortable, as we both breathed in the same air. Wild creatures don't like our strange human smell. It gives off a warning, because we are their enemy. Pa taught me that.

If I was to ask the creature to be my friend, I had to let her know that my humanness wasn't something to be frightened of. That people could be kind. That not all of us wanted to cut bits off her, like I'd seen Lady Cavendish try to do.

In the gloom, there was a rustle of vines. The creature waggled her huge ears and her coat of plants and trees rustled and rippled with her breathing. She blinked at me, as if waiting for me to do something.

We sat like that for a while, my back getting stiff against the cold brick wall.

"You really don't need to be frightened of me. I won't hurt you."

The creature extended her long nose towards me, like she'd done last night.

I paused, holding my breath.

She snuffled my clothes. My hair. My hands. I kept as still as possible, not wanting to make any sudden movements in case I scared her. She smelled of the forest floor, of moss and leaves and earth.

A blast of her breath warmed my face, then she curled her nose back around herself, like an eel retreating into the safety of the crevasse. She fluffed up her ferns and grassy coat and snuggled into a small ball.

My eyes began to feel heavy, and I yawned. Straw had been scattered on the cold brick floor, and I scrunched some into a pile and curled up. I didn't want to leave the pangea alone in the dark, by herself. Or maybe it was me who didn't want to be alone, who needed the company after a strange sort of day trying to work out the strange people who lived here.

"I'll stay here for a little bit," I yawned. "Just to keep you company."

The pangea snuffled, relaxing so that she wasn't so tightly curled up. In the torchlight, her eyes blinked at me, then closed. Soon, a gentle snore rumbled.

The creature needed a name. Studying her plants on her back, I was struck once again by the delicate ferns that curled and uncurled, apparently according to her mood. The ferns rose along her back when she was frightened, and they quivered, fanning out like a peacock's tail, when she was curious about something. Pa had once told me that fern plants are one of the oldest plants in the world. Ferns can even be found in the rocks, as fossils, and they remained unchanged and perfectly formed to this day.

"I'll call you Fern," I whispered, with another yawn. "Because just like the plant, you're magical and special and perfect."

*

I woke up, and the dark confused me. *Where was I?* The window that I usually woke up to, with its view of the gloomy clouds, was nowhere to be seen.

Plus, there was something close, something breathing.

I sat up and fumbled for my torch, switching it on with a snap.

Fern had moved closer to lie next to me on the floor, her sides gently rising with each breath. She was asleep, breathing deeply. I reached out and gently stroked her mossy side.

What time was it? Down here, it was hard to know.

I got up hurriedly and stretched the aches from my shoulder.

Fern stirred. Blinking up at me, she uncurled her trunk and pulled herself to stand.

"I really don't want to leave you." I patted the top of Fern's head. "I'll be back to visit later today, I promise."

I turned and left the room. The last thing I saw was Fern's eyes fixed on me, before the darkness swallowed her up.

Chapter 22

The Broken Lock

The door to the glasshouse was open. Too late, I realized I'd forgotten to lock the door last night, after the excitement of feeding the moonbirds. I cursed at my carelessness.

Griff was already inside. He was sitting on the path, very still, facing away from me.

To my surprise, he began to whistle, like I'd taught him. He whistled a few wheezy notes, gaining the attention of Echo, the macaw.

Echo swooped out of the treetops, landing with a flutter on the ground in front of Griff. I saw Griff's shoulders tense and his whistle quivered in fear.

I watched silently, holding my breath, waiting to see what Echo would do.

Griff held out an apple and Echo waddled over

to him, then snatched the apple from his hand and bounced away. Echo flapped up to his favourite tree and, using his claw, munched into the apple.

"That was brilliant!" I said, walking over.

Griff turned and squinted up at me. "I found some fallen apples this morning in the orchard. I thought Echo might like one."

"Are you less afraid of him now?" I asked gently.

Griff shrugged. "A bit." He looked uncertain. "I don't think I'm ready to feed the seacat, though!" He clambered to his feet.

"Of course not! You don't have to do anything that scares you. Creatures know when you're uncomfortable around them, which can make them feel afraid."

Griff pulled another apple from his pocket and held it out to me. "I got one for you too."

The apple was sweet and juicy and perfect for breakfast. We had fed the moonbirds and the pangolin the night before, and Griff had given Echo breakfast, so it was just the seacat and the glass dragon that needed feeding this morning.

We followed the path towards the seacat's enclosure. Butterflies swirled in the air currents as the glasshouse slowly warmed up, and the heavy smell of jasmine flowers tickled my nose. Then I thought of Fern, alone in the dark, and the shine went out of my beautiful surroundings. There must be some alternative to that dark room, some way we could safely bring the pangea outside into the sunlight and fresh air.

I suddenly felt a prickle of unease. Over Griff's shoulder, I spotted a pair of bright green eyes in the long reed grass, before they blinked and disappeared.

I tugged on Griff's arm. "There's something there, in the grass!" I whispered.

Griff went pale, his eyes wide. "What is it?" he hissed.

The eyes had been a familiar emerald green.

"Tempest." A wave of nausea swept over me. "Come on."

We sped around the corner to the seacat's enclosure and in a few hurried steps, my fears were confirmed.

The door to the enclosure was wide open.

I couldn't understand it. I had locked it the day before, after cleaning out the cage. Or had I? Doubts began to creep in around the edges of my mind.

I inspected the lock. It had fallen open, with

the shackle snapped off in the padlock. Could it have been an old lock? There was no sign of rust. I wracked my brains to try and remember if I'd locked the gate properly the day before, but I was wasting time. Right now, I had to focus on getting the seacat back into the enclosure.

"What are we going to do?" Griff clutched my arm, his whole body shaking. "It's going to eat us!"

"He's not going to eat us," I said, with as much confidence as I could muster. "We just need to come up with a plan."

The exit to the glasshouse was all the way at the other end, with a large wild cat between us and the door.

The seacat was really just a big cat, wasn't it? And all cats liked to chase; it was in their nature. I knew this from Crabbit chasing the crows in our garden on the farm.

"First, we mustn't run." I gently prised Griff's hand from my arm. "Do what I tell you, OK?"

Griff nodded. "Just don't let us get eaten."

"I promise," I said.

I looked around the glasshouse. "Look," I said to him quietly. "The food store has a lock. All we have to do is get inside there and we'll be safe."

He nodded again. Forcing myself to walk slowly, I guided us both along the path, keeping alert to any movement in the surrounding trees and shrubs. One step at a time. *Mustn't rush.* My palms were clammy and the air felt too stuffy to breath.

Griff whimpered next to me.

"Are you all right?" I asked him. "We're almost at the shed."

His eyes darted around anxiously. *Please don't run,* I begged him wordlessly.

After what seemed like an age, we made it to the shed. I unlocked it with trembling hands, while Griff kept a lookout.

I shoved the door open with my shoulder and pulled Griff inside.

I waited for his breathing to return to normal, then looked him in the eye. "Now, listen. I'm going to leave you in here and shut the door, OK, Griff? Don't panic, just sit tight and wait for me to tell you it's safe."

"But what are you going to do?" Griff cried. "You can't go back out there!"

"I have to! What if someone else comes into the glasshouse? What if something happens to the seacat? I need to get him back into the enclosure."

I closed the shed door behind me, and on impulse, I grabbed one of the spades leaning against the wall and propped it under the door handle. As afraid of the seacat as he was, I knew that Griff would try and help. I couldn't let him get hurt.

I had to figure out a plan, quickly.

I crept back down the path, towards where I'd seen the seacat, my legs trembling, every sound magnified. To my left, a twig cracked and I froze. Fear rose in my throat. I forced myself from breaking into a run back to the shed. I glanced to the side, where the trees grew close together, their long trunks stretching towards the glass ceiling. What had Lady Cavendish said? That the seacat was *a vicious, cruel beast*? I swallowed down the panic. As far as I'd seen, the seacat hadn't shown any signs of wanting to attack me, or Griff, and I felt we were beginning to form a bond. But he was a wild animal. I needed to be careful.

Slowing my breathing right down, I stood still next to the tall reed grass, in the spot where I'd seen him last.

I found myself staring at a face with blue and black stripes. The seacat. He peeked out from between the long green stalks of the reeds grass, only a leap away from me.

Tempest.

I shoved my hands in my pockets to keep them still, even though every inch of me was screaming to run.

I whistled softly, mimicking the twittering calls I'd heard Tempest make.

Chhhirrrrrrrrrrriiiiiipppppppp

The big cat blinked at me slowly. Instinctively, I blinked back, and Tempest yawned, showing devilishly sharp incisors.

Moistening my dry lips, I whistled again.

Chhhirrrrrrrrrrriiiiiipppppppp

Tempest suddenly padded out of the long grass and prowled towards where I was standing. I drew in a sharp breath.

Tempest strolled nearer and then, to my surprise, he purred. The vibrations of his deep voice shivered through the air. I stood as still as possible. He sauntered closer, then bumped me with his huge head, right on my shoulder, almost making me lose my balance.

The world seemed to stop as the fearsome creature purred and nudged me, playful as a kitten. I felt weak with relief and excitement, my legs trembling. Without the bars of the cage between us, I could see the flecks of gold in the seacat's eyes and the ripple of muscle beneath the blue and black fur. The talons on its huge webbed feet clicked on the pebble path, the sound magnified. I didn't feel afraid, not like I knew I should with a creature that could swipe my head off my shoulders. Instead, I felt an overwhelming sense of wonder.

But I still had to get him back in his enclosure.

Would he follow me? I wondered. I let my hands drop to the sides and began walking back towards the enclosure. After a moment, Tempest padded after me, his flattened tail flicking back and forth.

Once we reached the enclosure, I stepped aside, to let Tempest walk in, but he only sat down on his hind legs, his tail wrapped around his feet, and stared at me sullenly.

"You don't want to go back inside, do you?" I whispered.

I looked into the cage. It was too small. The

pond had already started to grow murky, with silt clouding the surface. No wonder the seacat was reluctant.

"I'm afraid you're going to have to go back in. I can't have you roaming around the glasshouse. What if someone sees you?" Mr Johnson would have a fit if he saw the big cat was loose. I glanced over my shoulder, half-expecting to see Mr Johnson already approaching. Luckily, it was just me and Tempest. For now.

The seacat whisked his tail. He blinked again, looking past me at the cage.

I remembered the fish that I had brought for Tempest's breakfast.

Bringing the large fish out of the barrow, I waved it in the air.

I threw the fish into the enclosure, where it landed with a wet *thump* on the hard dirt floor. The seacat sniffed the air, then strolled past me on his webbed feet, slinking through the open door and into the enclosure, where it tore into the fish with such gusto that I shivered. Improvising, I wrapped the chain around the door and the bars and propped it shut with the shovel. I would have to be more careful from now on. If something happened to one of the creatures, or anyone else, I don't know how I would forgive myself. Sensing the closed gate, Tempest glanced up from his feeding with a look of betrayal. I couldn't ignore how wrong it felt, taking advantage of the seacat's trust to trick and trap him back into his small cage. This wasn't what I thought being a creature keeper would be like. I felt like a villain.

The shed. Griff was still inside.

As soon as I opened the door, a red-faced Griff exploded out.

"That wasn't fair, Cora!" he yelled. "You shouldn't have locked me in there."

"I did it for your own good!" I protested. "It was dangerous with the seacat on the loose. I had to bring it back to the enclosure, without you getting hurt."

"I'm not your *pet* or a creature that needs looking after!" Griff shouted. "You had no right to lock me in that shed. I'm your *friend.* We take care of each other."

"I'm sorry," I said, hanging my head. I really was.

But Griff had already stormed off.

For the rest of the day, Griff avoided me. He didn't come anywhere near the glasshouse. He wasn't in the kitchen when I made myself a sandwich for lunch. Bea was nowhere to be seen, most probably somewhere in the house, battling the clutter. I suddenly felt very alone.

Before moving to Direspire Hall, I had been content with my animal and bird friends. I had never needed anyone else. But now I knew I had to make things right again with Griff. I couldn't bear the thought of him being angry with me. Another thought crept in: what if Griff never wanted to be friends with me again?

The clouds above Direspire Hall seemed particularly gloomy that afternoon. I found a brand-new padlock for the seacat's enclosure and made sure it was secure. I still found it odd that the lock would have snapped just like that. A sense of unease squeezed my chest. From now on, I'd make sure the enclosure was locked at all times.

After I had done my tasks, I headed upstairs to the attic, steering clear of Bea and Mr Johnson and Lady Cavendish. Griff was the only person I really wanted to see, and he was avoiding me.

The wind rattled the only window in the attic,

sending a cold draught scuttling around my bare feet. Even though it was summer, it felt wintery, with the clouds that stubbornly covered the top turrets of the house, night and day.

I waited until the house was quiet. And then, down the passageway I went.

This time, I brought blankets with me. I lit the lamp, filling the room with a warm glow. But the small room reminded me uneasily of the seacat's enclosure, and how I'd tricked him back into his cage, after his brief taste of almost-freedom. The feeling of unease deepened when I saw Fern.

She was curled in the corner, and didn't look up when I came in. In the lamplight, I could see that some of her leaves were wilting and fading. The ferns on her back were tinged with rust-coloured spots, and petals littered the floor.

"Oh, Fern," I whispered. "What's wrong?"

But I knew what was wrong. I had read it in *Creatures of the Four Realms*:

In darkness, the creature will remain undeveloped, but given the right conditions, fresh air and sunlight, the creature will grow rapidly, until it becomes an island, where it will eventually sustain an entire ecosystem of unique flora and fauna.

Fern needed sunlight to thrive.

I couldn't stop the tears welling up. I made a nest of blankets and curled up next to her, pressing my damp cheek to her mossy side. With everything that had happened today – Tempest escaping, his return to his small, cramped enclosure, and now Fern looking sick – I was beginning to wonder if I was the right person for the role.

I had thought that being the creature keeper of Direspire Hall would be the adventure I'd craved. I'd been trapped on the farm – but was it any better here? The creatures were just as trapped – and worst of all, I was their captor.

Chapter 23

The Graveyard

Lady Cavendish wasn't in her study when I knocked on the door the next morning.

"Do you know where Lady Cavendish is?" I asked Bea, who was sewing up a hole in one of Griff's shirts in the kitchen. Bea frowned. "I did see her early this morning, heading towards the orchard, but I haven't seen her return. She could still be there?"

I nodded my thanks and headed to the door, when Bea stopped me with a hand on my shoulder.

"Is everything all right, Cora?" she said gently. "Griff seems a little quiet. Have you two had an argument?" I didn't say anything. She brushed a stray curl behind her ear. "He's never really had the opportunity to spend much time with anyone his own age. We travelled while he was growing up and his pa..." Her voice trailed off. "I know that Griff has really enjoyed your company," she finished with a tiny smile.

My face heated up. I wish I could take back what I'd done. I wish I had never locked him in the store shed.

"Everything is fine, Bea," I reassured her. And it would be. I would make it all right.

But first, I had to speak to Lady Cavendish. I had to convince her to let me help Fern, by bringing her out of the cellar room and into the sunshine. I was sure this would help her heal, but I knew that time was running out.

I found Lady Cavendish in the orchard, as Bea had said. She was standing with her head lowered, her gaze fixed on something. At first I wasn't sure what she was looking at, then I saw the marble statue of an angel.

It was a gravestone.

"Lady Cavendish?" I said, walking up next to her. "Could I speak to you for a moment?"

Lady Cavendish spun around. "Cora, you startled me. What do you want?"

I glanced at the gravestone. It read: *Anne and William Cavendish. Together for ever.*

"It's the pangea," I said. "She isn't well. Her leaves are falling out and she looks sick."

"Do you know what happened to my parents?" Lady Cavendish interjected.

"No, but, Lady Cavendish..."

Again, Lady Cavendish cut me off. "I blamed the seacat for taking my parents away from me, but it was me that unlocked the door to the cage. I was older than you are now, Cora, but I didn't have your experience with animals. When my parents brought the creatures here, to Direspire Hall, I thought they would make great playthings. I opened the cage that day to pet it, like you would a cat. Although my parents were able to recapture the creature, it wasn't before the seacat managed to get in several swipes with its poison-tipped claws. They died soon after." Lady Cavendish sighed. "I often thought about getting rid of the creature."

I thought of the seacat which had purred and nudged me so playfully yesterday. But Tempest was older now, his muzzle grey. Once he had been younger, wilder.

"I kept the seacat, because I know that is what

my parents would have wanted. They risked everything to bring the creatures here, and to get rid of them would have been a waste of all their hard work. My parents had always hoped that Direspire Hall would become a place of learning, and the study of extraordinary creatures. But I couldn't bear the thought of another accident happening, so I shut Direspire for good."

"You might wonder why I'm telling you this now, Cora." Lady Cavendish turned to me. "I want you to remember that these are wild creatures. They are not farm animals or pets. They are dangerous."

"But Lady Cavendish, Fern isn't well. Her leaves are falling off the tree on her back, and her flowers are wilting. I don't know what to do." The words hiccupped out of me and I felt my eyes well up.

"Fern?" Lady Cavendish said, with a raised eyebrow. "You've named the creature?"

I nodded. Of course I had.

"I never named them. It just seemed so arbitrary to name the creatures, as they were specimens to be studied, a small part of the invaluable research to which my parents gave their lives." Lady Cavendish plucked a patch of moss off the gravestone and threw it to the ground. "I don't want you to let the creature, or *Fern*, if you will, leave the basement. She needs to adjust to the lack of light. Darkness never killed anyone before." Lady Cavendish turned to go back to Direspire Hall, leaving me in the orchard.

Frustrated tears spilled out and I dug my hands deep into my pockets, clenching them until my nails cut painfully into my palms.

I wiped the tears away. I was never going to convince Lady Cavendish. I would have to take matters into my own hands. Slowly, a plan began to form.

First, I needed to find Griff.

I found him in the glasshouse, sitting cross-legged and feeding the tortoises with lettuce leaves.

I sat down next to him. One of the tortoises ambled over and peered up at me, stretching out its leathery-looking neck. I scratched the top of its head and the tortoise closed its eyes with a look of contentment.

"I'm sorry I locked you in the shed yesterday," I said to Griff. "I was trying to keep you safe, but I know *now* that I should have trusted you."

He didn't look at me. "Yes, you should have trusted me. Do you know what that was like, getting locked in the shed like I was an animal? It was horrible. It reminded me of when my pa would lock me in the cart."

I hadn't even thought of that. The guilt stung even more.

"I'm really sorry, Griff," I said. "That was thoughtless. And – and I understand if you don't want to be friends any more."

Griff grinned, wrinkling his freckled nose. "Don't be stupid," he said. "Of course I want to be friends!"

"You do?" I wiped my nose with my sleeve.

Griff rolled his eyes. "Of course. You said sorry, didn't you? Well, then."

A warm feeling settled in my stomach. We were still friends. I still had a friend. Then I decided.

"Griff," I said. "I need your help."

"With what?" Griff asked, his eyes curious.

"I can't really explain; I'll have to show you. Can you sneak away tonight and meet me in the attic? There is someone I'd like you to meet."

The rest of the day went by quickly. We tended to the animals and then sat by the seacat's enclosure, whistling to Tempest, who appeared to enjoy the attention, rubbing his face against the bars and purring loudly. Griff even managed to feed Tempest his meal of fish, poking it through the bars, which surprised me and him.

"He's just like a big cat," Griff smiled. "I don't think he really wants to eat me."

"You still have to be careful," I cautioned, Lady Cavendish's warning echoing in my ears. "He's a wild animal."

"All right, I know," said Griff, in mock exasperation. "But I'm getting better at creature keeping, aren't I?"

"You are!" I laughed. It felt good to be friends with Griff again. I was glad he was on my side. And I knew I'd need him if I wanted to help Fern.

Chapter 24

New Friends

It took ages for Direspire Hall to quieten for the night, but finally I heard creaky footsteps on the stairs.

"Cora?" Griff whispered through the attic door. "Are you there?"

I let him into the attic. "This way!" I'd opened the secret door in preparation. I clambered inside, before switching my torch on and illuminating the way ahead.

Griff hesitated. "What's down there?" He narrowed his eyes. "Am I going to get in trouble?"

"Not if you're quiet!" I motioned for him to follow. "Quick!"

I led the way down the stairwell, my torch sweeping over the small space. When we arrived at Lady Cavendish's door, her light was still on. I pressed my finger to my lips and Griff nodded.

Down the stairs we went, until we reached the underground passageway.

"This is where Lady Cavendish keeps her," I told Griff, sweeping the light down the long corridor. There was no sound from her room, and a niggling sense of unease settled in my chest.

"Who does she keep here?" Griff's voice wobbled. "Cora?"

I hurried down the corridor, with Griff close behind.

"You have to promise not to get scared, OK?" Then I opened the door.

I called out to Fern.

Herrroooooooooooooooooooaaaaahhhhhooooo

Fern trotted over, picking her legs up high, just like our old horse Merlin. She halted just in front of us, her ferns flattened against her back. She raised her nose in a question mark.

"Lift your palm out, Griff, so that she can take a good sniff of you."

Griff trembled, but slowly lifted his hand into

the air. Fern lowered her nose and prodded his hand.

Griff gasped. He stared at Fern, his mouth gaped open in surprise. "There are plants growing on her back! Is that a tree?"

"Yes, she's an island! Or at least, she will be eventually, I think, if she's allowed to grow. I've named her Fern."

"An island?" Griff sucked in his breath. "Why has Lady Cavendish kept this a secret?"

"Fern only hatched recently. She's extremely rare, and Lady Cavendish is afraid that someone might steal her away. If Fern is in the sunlight she will grow and grow, until she's huge." Griff nodded, his eyes wide and serious. "But she's not growing at all here, in the dark. Look, her plants are all dying." I pointed out the withering vines and the littering of dead flowers on the floor, among the straw. "We have to get her out of here, and bring her to the glasshouse, where she'll have fresh air and sunlight. Just until she's well again."

"Lady Cavendish will find out." Griff nibbled his thumbnail.

"I can't leave her here, Griff. Will you help me?"

"I can't," Griff said. "What if she kicks Ma and

me out? We have nowhere else to go. You can go back to your farm, at least."

I pressed my face against Fern's back. She smelled of autumn now, the too-sweet smell of fallen leaves. How much longer did she have? Her eyes were dull, and the tree on her back had lost all but one of its leaves.

"I'm getting her out of here," I said firmly. "Whether you help or not. I don't want to get you in trouble – but I have to do this. Tonight."

Chapter 25
The Escape

There was a long pause, in which Griff and I looked at each other over Fern's bowed head.

"I shouldn't have pressured you to help," I finally admitted. It wasn't fair to ask Griff to help me, not when he had so much to lose. "I've just felt so confused recently, about the creatures. It feels wrong, keeping them locked up, in small cages. The seacat should have the whole ocean to explore, instead of a pond. The moonbirds are trapped in a glass box. And Fern..." I stroked Fern's nose. "She stuck down here, in a dark room, all alone."

"As the creature keeper, I have to do what's right for Fern, and Tempest, and all the other creatures." *Even if it means breaking the rules.*

"OK," sighed Griff. "I'll help you."

"Are you sure?" I said. "I really don't want you to get into trouble."

He lifted his chin. "I'll be all right," he told me.

I grinned at him. "Follow us, Fern," I told her.

I opened the door and stepped back into the narrow passageway.

Fern stayed in the room, her eyes wide and fearful.

"Come along, Fern, you can do it! We haven't got much time!" I strained to hear any sounds from the floor above us.

But Fern didn't want to follow.

In desperation, I called to her in her own words.

Herrroooooooooooooooooooaaaaahhhhhooooo

She took a step forward, then hesitated. "I know it's scary, but you can do it, Fern," I whispered, as she took another step forward. "Just follow me."

And then suddenly, Fern did, her ears flapping anxiously.

Step by small step, we walked up the passageway, with Fern close behind. We came to the trapdoor that led out to the garden, where tendrils of mist snaked across the dewy grass. The sky was dawn-pink.

"Come on, Fern. Just a few more steps." I coaxed, holding the trapdoor open for her.

Fern put one webbed foot on the grass, delicately probing at the stalks with her trunk, then she took another step, until she'd walked out into the open. Griff closed the trapdoor behind her.

With one hand on her side, I guided Fern towards the glasshouse. We made slow progress, as Fern stopped to scoop soil from the flower beds up in her trunk. She flung the soil over her head in a shower of dirt.

"Watch where you're throwing that!" Griff scolded her, shaking the clods of dirt from his hair, but there was a smile in his voice.

Fern's tail wriggled, like a lamb.

"Look how happy she is!" I caught my laugh in my hands, and glanced up at Direspire Hall. The windows were dark. "Let's get her inside the glasshouse, before anyone wakes up."

When we got to the glasshouse, Fern trotted in after me and Griff and I locked the door behind her with a sigh of relief. I felt safe for now, knowing that I was the only one with keys to get in and out.

In the heat of the glasshouse, Fern's plants spread out and soon gleamed with vapour droplets. She stretched and sighed, letting out a harrumph.

A harsh *caw* and Echo the macaw soared through the air. With a swoop, he landed on the tree in the middle of Fern's back. He bobbed his head up and down, tapping out a dance on the branch.

"What are you doing up there?" I laughed, surprised that the macaw had chosen Fern's tree, when he was usually very particular about perching in the cherry trees.

"Echo, Echo!" the macaw taunted me, before twirling and fluffing out his feathers, then settling down contentedly.

It appeared he was intent on staying where he was. Griff stood next to me. "I can't believe she's real!" he said. "Are you sure she won't hurt us? She doesn't have poisonous breath or fangs?"

"I don't think so." *Creatures of the Four Realms* hadn't mentioned fangs or poison. "She's got sharp claws, but she won't attack you unless you try and prune her."

"Prune her?" Griff patted Fern, running his hands over the moss on her shoulders.

I told Griff about Lady Cavendish's attempt at pruning Fern's leaves. "It just seemed really cruel." I hoped there would be no need to prune Fern. How fast could she really grow anyway?

Griff yawned. "I'll head back, before Ma wakes up."

"Thank you for your help, Griff." It was such a relief to have Fern out of that dark room, and Griff had risked a lot to help me.

I said goodbye to Griff at the glasshouse door.

"I'm staying with Fern tonight," I said. "I don't want her to get lonely, in a new place."

Besides, with the way that Mr Johnson was usually skulking around, I wanted to make sure she was safe. I only hoped that I'd made the right decision, bringing her out here.

Chapter 26
Unfurling

I woke up, curled up on the sackcloth I'd found in the shed.

I staggered to my feet. "Fern!" I called. It was late morning now, and the bright sun stabbed my sleep-crusted eyes. "Where are you?" If she'd somehow managed to escape the glasshouse, I was in big trouble.

A sloshing, slurping noise came from the direction of the seacat's enclosure. The feeling of unease deepened.

Taking a detour through the bamboo plants, I found Fern.

To my shock, she had managed to reach her trunk through the bars of the enclosure, and was slurping the seawater from Tempest's pond, before reaching her trunk into her mouth and gulping it down.

But where was Tempest? Then I spotted him. Instead of being furious at the intrusion, he was rubbing his head up against Fern's trunk, a deep purr rumbling from his chest.

Fern stopped her swigging from the pond, to nudge the large cat with her trunk, as affectionately as I would pat Crabbit the cat. It appeared the two sea-dwelling creatures were natural friends.

That wasn't the only surprise. Fern's foliage had already grown back, the vines sprouting new leaves and soft green moss had spread across her sides. The petals on the tiny daisies that dotted the grassy meadow on her shoulders unfurled to the sun. There were bright blue and red and yellow tulips, and vines curled down to the ground. Red leaves grew on the branches of her tree, and patches of long grass had emerged, that swayed with every step. I could even see two tiny protruding tusks emerging on either side of her mouth, with delicate creeping vines growing around them.

And she was growing bigger. She had already doubled in size, and was bigger than Merlin, our old cart horse. It was astonishing how quickly she was able to grow, now that she had fresh air and sunlight. I still hadn't come up with a plan to keep her here, but for now, it made me happy to see Fern flourishing.

While I went about my creature-keeping duties, Fern trotted after me, like the faithful dog I'd always wanted. She seemed curious of the moonbirds, prodding the glass with her trunk, as they slumbered, huddled in cloud-like groups. I loved having her company while Griff was busy gardening and I found myself talking to her.

"Next, the pangolin burrow," I told Fern. There wasn't really a way of checking on the pangolin during the day, but I filled her bowl with clean water in case she got thirsty in the meantime.

Outside the seacat's enclosure, I whistled for Tempest. Fern snuffled at the bars.

Tempest slunk out of the pond and padded over. He nuzzled the bars and purred, a sound like gravel underfoot. He seemed curious about Fern, mesmerized by her. In her presence, he became almost kittenish, bouncing along as he followed her from behind the bars of the cage.

"I've got your breakfast, Tempest." I held the fish through the bars of the enclosure.

The blue-and-black striped seacat snatched the fish out of my hand and sloped back to his pond. With hardly a ripple, he disappeared under the water.

"Shall we go and see Brittle?" I asked Fern. It was strange having a companion that looked like a walking allotment. Even stranger that there was a jewel-coloured macaw sitting comfortably in the tree on her back.

We crossed the bridge, over the pond where the perch lurked.

"Hello, Brittle," I called out. "How are you today?"

I pressed my nose against the glass. My breath fogged.

Inside the enclosure, the mist stirred. In the swirl, the bat-winged creature soared. By now, my eyes were quicker to catch the shape of the nearly-invisible dragon.

Brittle spun through the air, round and round.

And, just then, a banging on the door of the glasshouse made me jump.

Chapter 27
Found Out

With shaking hands, I unlocked the glasshouse and came face to face with a furious Lady Cavendish.

She was clutching a paintbrush, which she brandished wildly. "I was in the middle of painting a new portrait, when I decided to check on the pangea." There were two pinpricks of red in her cheeks. "Imagine my surprise, Cora, when I discovered the room empty."

Lady Cavendish pushed past, knocking me out of the way. "Where is she? I'm taking her back down to the cellar room immediately."

Drawn by the commotion, Fern trotted into sight, her trunk raised in a question mark.

Stopping in her tracks, all the colour drained from Lady Cavendish's face. "Look at the size of her!" she spluttered. "You haven't been pruning her at all, have you, Cora?" She took another angry step forward, her dark eyes flashing.

That was the wrong thing to do. Fern leaped forward with a deafening howl that shook the panes of the glasshouse. The cherry trees trembled with the noise, sending a snowstorm of petals into the air. Fern looked fearsomely huge and otherworldly.

"What have you done, Cora?" Lady Cavendish gasped. "The beast has grown into a monster, too large and too powerful. We'll never be able to contain her."

Fern wasn't a monster. I needed Lady Cavendish to realize that. If she was afraid, she would only find a way of cutting bits off Fern and locking her away.

Taking a deep breath, I filled my lungs and:

Herrrooooooooooooooooooaaaaahhhhhooooo

I called out to Fern, telling her that everything was all right. Although my noise didn't rattle the windows or shake the cherry trees, the effect on Fern was instant. Her hackles fell and she flapped her ears.

I went to greet her, pressing my hand against

her mossy flank and stroking her long nose. "It's all right. Lady Cavendish wants to be friends. Don't you, Lady Cavendish?" I beckoned her over.

Lady Cavendish blinked, startled. Then she tucked the paintbrush in her pocket and inched forward, towards Fern.

With my heart in my mouth, I watched as Lady Cavendish patted the wildflower meadow on Fern's shoulders, the tiny flowers bending under her palm.

Curious, Fern sniffed Lady Cavendish's hair with her trunk, fiddling with the paintbrush she'd stuck in her pocket. My heart swelled with pride for Fern, and relief at how quickly she had forgiven Lady Cavendish for pruning her and keeping her in the basement.

Seeing Fern toying with the paintbrush gave me a flash of inspiration. The blank pages at the end of *Creatures of the Four Realms* were intended to be filled with pictures of the pangea.

"Your ma and pa would want you to draw the pangea," I said. "To add to their research."

Lady Cavendish scoffed. "Don't be daft," she said.

I grew bold. "If you're only going to draw your ma

and pa, how are you going to be able to document the extraordinary creatures they brought back here and carry on their legacy?"

It was quiet for a long moment, as we both petted Fern, who seemed perfectly happy with the attention, as long as there were no shears in sight. "Maybe you're right, Cora," Lady Cavendish said softly. "There is no harm in attempting to paint the creature, for posterity reasons. If my parents were still alive, they wouldn't let this opportunity go to waste. The pangea can stay in the glasshouse for now. At least, until I've managed to paint her, then we'll see about what to do with her next."

"Do you promise not to prune her?" I whispered.

Lady Cavendish dipped her head in agreement. "I promise," she said. "At least for now."

While Lady Cavendish headed back to Direspire Hall to collect her art supplies, I busied myself setting up a space for her to paint, sweeping the leaves off the path.

"You're going to get your portrait painted, Fern! You'd better be on your best behaviour!" I sang, my heart soaring. "And you, Echo!" I called up to the bird on the tree on Fern's back. The glasshouse was warm and cosy, and my head was full of plans for the day. I was going to start exploring how we could build a bigger enclosure for Tempest and the moonbirds, and where I could search for the tastiest grubs for Pinecone the pangolin.

I heard a noise coming from the entrance and turned. "Griff?" I called out. "Lady Cavendish?"

A figure came into view. Mr Johnson. Taking in the sight of Fern, his eyes shone, like a wolf scenting blood.

"What do we have here?" His mouth stretched into a grin that looked jarring against his usually sour face. "This is certainly a surprise addition to the menagerie."

Something about his expression worried me. It was greedy. I thought of Mr Johnson's strange appearances, at odd times of the day and night; as if he'd been looking for something, or waiting for something to happen.

Now, his cold eyes gleamed.

"You've been very conscientious about locking the glasshouse, and I can see why." Mr Johnson tilted his head. "Lady Cavendish failed to mention the existence of this creature to me. How long have you been keeping this a secret?"

I kept my mouth shut. Fern was none of his business.

"No matter," Mr Johnson chuckled. "Just keep the creature here, where it can do no harm." He abruptly turned and walked away, towards the entrance, until the cherry trees obscured him from view.

Quick as a mouse, I padded after him. He was up to something; I knew it in my bones. And this time, I was going to see what it was.

Chapter 28
Stranger at the Gate

Mr Johnson scurried out of the glasshouse, heading straight to Direspire Hall.

I locked the glasshouse behind me and I followed at a distance, keeping to the trees. Instead of turning towards the house, Mr Johnson headed towards the gate. I trailed behind, under cover of the overgrown shrubbery.

At the gate, Mr Johnson glanced over his shoulder, sweeping his eyes towards Direspire Hall, while I ducked into the brambles, getting as close as I dared, ignoring the thorns prickling my skin. Seemingly satisfied he was alone, Mr Johnson whistled through the gate, the two notes of a cuckoo call.

Almost immediately, as if he'd been skulking

nearby, a man appeared on the other side of the gate. This time, I had a better view. He wore snake-skin shoes and velvet trousers, and he had sleek blonde hair combed into a severe middle parting. His eyes were such a pale blue they appeared almost white, and gave him an eerie, shrewd look. There was a faint sniff of the familiar about him.

The wind ruffled his blonde hair, briefly teasing the severe parting into an untidy mop, before the man smoothed it back down.

"My price has doubled," Mr Johnson barked through the bars. "And it'll be worth every penny and more."

"Doubled? You must be joking!" the stranger laughed, which turned Mr Johnson's ears red. "It would have to be a golden goose for that kind of money."

Try as I might, I couldn't catch any more of the hushed words exchanged between the two men, but Mr Johnson must have said something compelling, because the man smiled triumphantly, making his thin moustache twitch like a fish caught on a hook. As quickly as he'd appeared, he strode away, vanishing behind the great stone wall of Direspire Hall, towards the moors. Mr Johnson turned towards Direspire again, with a swagger in his walk.

Something about the man bothered me, an itch that I couldn't quite scratch. Then I knew why that man on the other side of the gates seemed so familiar.

As the wind had ruffled his hair, I had been staring right at Griff's wild shock of blonde hair.

I found Griff in the orchard, teetering precariously on a ladder.

"Griff!" I panted, out of breath from running all the way. "Do you have a picture of you pa?" I didn't want to scare him without knowing if I was right.

Griff wrinkled his nose, with a look of bewilderment, but he nodded. "I'll show you if you like." He wobbled down the ladder, with a basket of apples over his arm. "Do you need to see it right now?"

I nodded. "I'll explain in a minute."

Griff's room was neat and tidy, with only a small suitcase in the corner. He went over to the suitcase and began rummaging through the clothes.

Griff caught me frowning at the packed suitcase.

"I didn't want to jinx it," he said quietly.

I felt a rush of anger towards his pa. No one should have to keep their suitcase packed, out of fear. Griff's pa was stealing away his right to a home.

"Don't tell Ma that I've still got this," Griff said, pulling out a folded piece of paper. "I don't know why I keep it; it only brings up bad memories. But maybe that's why I do. It reminds me that things can change and get better."

I unfolded the paper in my hand, and my worst fears were realized.

It was a poster, advertising *Charles Linton's Marvellous Travelling Menagerie!* And there was a picture of the man underneath, the same man I'd seen at the gates, wearing the same snakeskin boots.

I scanned the rest of the poster. *Get your fortune told by the mystic chicken! Marvel at the magical unicorn! And gasp at THE GREAT CRUSTACEAN!* I peered at the terrifying drawing of the great crustacean itself, with its spider-like legs and armoured body, and realized something else.

It was the same drawing I'd seen in *Creatures of the Four Realms*.

The Great Crustacean was a fossil-feeder, from the Deep Earth, capable of grinding down bones with its vicious jaws.

I stared at Griff in dismay. "There's something I need to tell you, Griff. Your pa – he's here."

Bea smoothed the poster out on to the kitchen table with trembling fingers.

"I told Cora about Pa and why we're here, Ma," Griff said. "She's my friend and I trust her." His face was pinched with dread.

Bea didn't take her eyes off the poster on the table. "Are you sure you saw this man, Cora?"

I nodded.

"But how did he find us?" Griff burst out. "We haven't left Direspire Hall, no one has."

"Mr Johnson overheard us, talking about your pa," I said, suddenly remembering that day in the glasshouse. "Could he have gone to Brambury to find him? I saw him leave Direspire Hall that night, dressed in his overcoat and walking boots." I wished I'd said something sooner.

"I never did trust that man." Bea rubbed her freckled nose, looking exhausted. "For the moment, we're as safe as we can be, in Direspire Hall. The gates are locked." She didn't sound sure, though, and her forehead was wrinkled with worry. "But if Charles knows we're here, and if he knows about

271

the extraordinary creatures, we'll never be able to rest easy. We'll have to leave, Griff. You know he will do anything to get to the creatures, and he'll find a way to take us back."

"I don't *want* to leave!" Griff sounded close to tears, and I felt my own eyes start to prickle. I didn't want him to leave either.

What could I possibly say to ease the trapped-rabbit fear that I saw in Griff's pinched face? No words felt right.

The only person I could think of who might be able to help was Lady Cavendish. The last time I'd seen her, she was heading to her study to collect her painting things.

I ducked out of the kitchen, leaving Bea and Griff talking in low tones.

Out in the hallway, I heard banging. *Thud thud thud.* It came from upstairs.

I raced up the stairs, and along the upstairs hallway. Her door was shut.

Thud thud thud.

I knocked on the door. "Lady Cavendish?"

"Cora!" came the muffled, and outraged, reply. "I've been locked in!"

"By who?" My question was answered by a heavy hand on my shoulder.

Mr Johnson, his lips pressed together in a scowl.

Chapter 29
Locked In

Up the stairs Mr Johnson dragged me, his grip like a vice.

"You should have left when you had the chance." Mr Johnson shoved me into the attic. "I gave you plenty of opportunities, even sabotaging one of the enclosures, in the hope you would do what any clever person would and leave this place for good."

"It was you!" I gasped, with sudden understanding. "You let the seacat out of his cage!" He'd put everyone in danger, including Tempest.

I spun around with a surge of fury in my chest, but the door slammed shut behind me. The key clicked in the lock.

A sickly feeling of panic took hold of me, and

I threw my fists against the door, shaking it in its frame.

I pressed my ear against the door and listened.

Far below, there was a slam of a door. I caught a snatch of muffled voices, then a scream that was sharply silenced. The foreboding feeling dug its claws into my chest.

I pushed myself away from the door and darted to the window. If I stood on the tips of my toes, I could make out three trailers parked up near the gates of Direspire, the kind of trailers used to transport livestock. They hadn't been there before.

Whatever Mr Johnson and Charles Linton were up to I knew that we'd need back-up. Taking the lamp out of my bag, I lit it and placed it in the window. From here, I could see Bill's croft. I just hoped he would see the signal and be able to raise the alarm with Ma and Pa.

Luckily, Mr Johnson didn't know about the secret passageway. I put my bag over my shoulder, then grappled with the edge of the door in the wall, prising it open. Sticking my head into the dark interior, I listened, tilting my head to the side to catch any sign of intruders. The silence was deafening. A whiff of damp floated on the air.

Once inside the passageway, I pulled the door shut. If Mr Johnson came to check on me, I didn't want him to know where I was. Or where I was going.

I switched my torch on, but it held the light for only a moment, before flickering and going dead, plunging me back into darkness.

"Not now," I groaned. Banging it against my hand didn't help. I dropped the torch back into my bag.

I'd walked down the stairs enough times to know where I was going. I would just have to be careful not to trip.

My progress was painfully slow and I didn't dare hurry. The spiral passageway seemed far steeper in complete darkness, and I soon felt dizzy and disorientated.

I was all too aware of how loud and fast my breathing was. Then suddenly I heard more breathing, out of sync with mine. Air breathed in and hissed out.

Someone was here with me, in the pitch-black.

Two things happened very quickly.

I collided into someone and got an elbow or a knee jammed into my stomach, knocking the wind from my belly, and we both lost our footing.

In a heap, we tumbled down the stairs, all knotted and tangled up limbs and shouted curses.

I landed on something soft at the bottom of the stairs.

"Get off me," a woman gasped. "Crook! Villain! You won't get away with this."

"Lady Cavendish?" I rolled to the side. "Is that you?"

"Cora?" Lady Cavendish's voice softened. She got to her feet. "Arthur betrayed me." Her voice was hollow, then it hardened. "He locked me in my study while I was gathering my paints and canvases. I heard a commotion from downstairs, Bea and Griff..." She trailed off. "Something has happened to them."

I told her about the man I'd seen Mr Johnson talking to at the gates. Griff's pa, Charles Linton. "I think he's after the creatures, as well as Bea and Griff."

"I should have been more aware of what was going on, right under my nose. I shouldn't have been so trusting of Arthur, even after all these years."

The horrible, sickly feeling in my stomach returned.

"We have to help them!" I pressed my hand

against the wall, steadying myself. "We can get out through the trap door into the garden."

"Very well; you lead the way, Cora."

I crept forward, making my way down the corridor. I knew from the familiar smell of flowers and leaves, that we were passing Fern's old room. *Fern.* I tried not to think about what might be happening outside. Would the creatures be safe in the glasshouse?

Together, Lady Cavendish and I pushed the trapdoor open. The sunlight blinded me for a moment, after being in the dark. Outside, the wind howled and grey clouds hung low above. It was unseasonably cold.

Lady Cavendish let the trapdoor drop with a clang. "Let's find that rogue Arthur, and that coward Charles Linton."

But I couldn't speak. Shock froze me still.

From here, I could see the glasshouse, or what was left of it.

The magnificent building was only steel bones, the glass in shattered pieces on the ground.

Chapter 30
Broken Glass

The glass crunched underfoot as we ran.

"Fern's gone!" I cried. I scanned the area, looking for clues.

The plants had been trampled, squashed into the ground. Snapped branches and broken flowers littered the pebble path, all jumbled up with shards of glittering glass.

"The pangolin has been dug up from its burrow," said Lady Cavendish, leaning over the enclosure. "It's as if this man Charles knew exactly what he was looking for; it was all done too quickly."

As if he'd been summoned, Charles Linton appeared from around the corner of Direspire Hall, followed by Mr Johnson, and a woman who had a squirrelly look about her, clever and sharp.

My blood curdled at the sight of Mr Johnson. If the butler felt any shame at all in betraying Lady Cavendish, his dour face didn't show it.

Lady Cavendish strode towards the group. "Arthur, how could you betray me like this? I trusted you!"

Mr Johnson scoffed. "Oh sure, you trust me to get your shopping and make your tea, paying me a pittance for the pleasure while allowing this mere child to act as your creature keeper. Thankfully, Mr Linton is willing to pay me what I'm worth."

Before she could reply, Charles stepped forward and extended his arms wide, as if delighted to see her. "Lady Cavendish! I was under the impression you were tucked up safe and sound in Direspire Hall. But it appears you know the place far better than me, or your loyal butler." His thin moustache twitched as he spoke, as if it wanted to jump right off his mean-looking face.

Lady Cavendish's voice rang out, loud and defiant. "You will bring me back my creatures and pay for the damage to my property!"

"You're hardly one to talk about stealing, given the way you've been hiding my family away from me," spat Charles. "And your creatures will be much better off with me than they are in this crumbling old house."

I shivered. The three thieves didn't look the sort to feel threatened by Lady Cavendish, a grey-haired lady wearing a ratty pair of dungarees and a scowl.

I was right. Quick as a terrier, the woman sprang towards Lady Cavendish and wrestled her arms behind her back. Lady Cavendish squawked in outrage.

"Grab that little sprite as well." Charles Linton nodded at me.

I spun on my heels, but Mr Johnson was surprisingly quick. He swung out his leg, tripping me, and had my arms pinned painfully behind my back before I could take a breath.

Charles clapped his hands sharply. "Put them in one of the trailers, where they'll be out of the way until we're finished here. We'll drop them off somewhere on the moors, once we're far enough away."

As we were shoved towards the gates of Direspire, I could only hope that Bill would see the lamp that I'd lit in the attic window and raise the alarm, before it was too late.

Chapter 31
Trapped

Three livestock trailers were parked up on the moor, just off the road that led past Bill's croft, where smoke curled upwards from the chimney. It was the same road that continued into the middle of town.

Mr Johnson pushed me forward, towards the closest trailer.

"Fern!" I cried out when I saw her. A heavy chain had been locked around her neck and secured to the trailer at the front of the convoy. She rocked from side to side, her trunk swinging in agitation. On the tree on her back, Echo squawked loudly, a look of fury in his beady eyes.

Mr Johnson unlocked the padlock to the last trailer and shoved me inside, with Lady Cavendish close behind. The door slammed shut, and I heard the clink of the padlock being locked back into position.

The dark interior smelled of damp straw and animal dung.

The trailer was as big as a small barn, damp and dark. Now I *really* knew how Fern and the other creatures felt, trapped behind bars with no escape.

"Cora!" Griff crawled over to me out of the darkness and pulled me to my feet. "Are you all right?"

Lady Cavendish rubbed her wrists. "I am sorry, all of you," she said, her voice low. "I trusted Arthur and look what has happened. I have put you all in danger, and now he's taken one of the most priceless creatures that ever lived."

"It's my fault." I jammed my hands in my pockets. "I was the one that brought Fern out of the basement and into the glasshouse. I put her in danger."

Bea took hold of Lady Cavendish's hands. "He tricked all of us, and brought Charles here." She reached out and grabbed hold of my hand and I took Griff's, so that we were in a circle. "We're going to have to stick together and find a way to get out of here."

I nodded. "We can't let him take the creatures." The memory of Fern chained up made me feel sick to my stomach.

"I managed to save one of the creatures," said Griff, rather shyly. "I took her from the crate they'd put her in, when they were busy with Fern. It's all I could do. Look."

He pulled back his jumper and there was Pinecone, curled against his chest.

My heart swelled with pride. "That was really brave," I told him. "Now we have to make sure we rescue the others, together."

Outside, I could hear the sounds of activity. Chains clinking and doors being slammed.

In the door of the trailer we were being held in, there were bars that I could see out of but couldn't reach my hand through. I pressed my face against the metal, blinking against the sudden chill of the moorland wind.

I watched in dismay as Mr Johnson wheeled a metal crate through the gates of Direspire Hall, with Tempest inside. The seacat cowered and snarled in the corner of the cage. Charles brandished a whip, using it to direct Mr Johnson. The vicious-looking cane had leather strips wrapped around it, with metal embedded in knots on the end that clinked as he walked. At the sight of it, Tempest hissed, his ears flat against his skull.

"Put the cat in the last trailer, next to the crustacean," said Charles. "We'll have another search for the glass dragon, but I want to be moving on as quickly as possible." The three of them headed back into Direspire Hall.

I sank back down and pressed my forehead against the wood. I felt helpless, trapped – like the animals of Direspire Hall. Lady Cavendish wanted to protect the creatures from the world, while Charles Linton only wanted to make money from them, but neither Charles or Lady Cavendish put the happiness of the creatures first.

I had to get Fern's attention. If I could get her to come closer, maybe there was a way we could use her strength to escape.

Taking a deep breath, I hollered out of the opening.

I called out to her, singing our language, telling her where I was.

Reaching up to the bars on the window, I saw Fern lift her head in our direction, her trunk in a question mark. I cried out with all my might, willing my voice to reach Fern.

Griff joined in, calling through the bars, but it wasn't enough. The wind frayed our voices.

To my surprise, Lady Cavendish stood too, joining me, sending a howl through the small window.

Herrrooooooooooooooooooooaaaaahhhhhooooo

Then a third voice joined us. Bea.
We hollered together.

Herrrooooooooooooooooooooaaaaahhhhhooooo

Fern bellowed. She snuffled at the air and caught our scent.

She lurched forward, towards our trailer, her mossy face growing larger with each step. The chain clanked tighter around her neck, tearing up the delicate flowers that bloomed there.

You're so much stronger than you know, Fern! I willed her towards me.

The trailer rocked as Fern pressed her face against the small window. I could smell the earth and crushed flowers. Her breath exhaled. *I'm here, Fern.* I pressed my face to the opening. A vine tickled my cheek.

Carefully, I hooked my finger around the plant. *If we could wrap it around the metal bars, maybe Fern could break us free?*

I pulled the thick stems through the opening, weaving them around the bars, like threads on a loom. Lady Cavendish gave a gasp of understanding and began to do the same. The wagon grew dark, as we weaved the vines around the bars, blocking out the sunlight.

Finally, I banged my hand against the side of the wagon. "Pull, Fern!" I shouted. "You can do it!" Griff's eyes shone in the dark of the trailer, as we both watched in amazement as Fern grasped the bars firmly and started to pull. I could feel the excitement build like a kettle full of steam.

"Go on, Fern!" We both shouted encouragements, as the wooden door gave a groan.

The vines constricted around the bars. Then a crack. I shielded my eyes, as the wood splintered and sunlight poured into the cart.

"Quickly!" Griff grabbed my arm.

The cart door had been torn off its hinges and

Lady Cavendish kicked away the splintered boards. She jumped clear of the cart, before helping Bea down. I leaped down and ran to Fern.

Griff bounced towards me, leaping over the grass like a frog out of the pond, his arms wrapped protectively around his middle, where the pangolin snuggled.

"Look who's also here!" He pointed upwards. "She must have slipped right past them."

Silently circling above Fern, I caught sight of a familiar ripple of bat-like wings in the clouds. *Brittle.*

"I bet they're still looking for an invisible dragon in the empty enclosure," Griff chuckled. "Serves them right,"

I laid my hand on Fern's trunk. I wasn't going to let Charles take her away.

"What the devil's going on here, then?" Bill appeared, with Maisie trotting alongside him. She wagged her tail furiously when she saw me.

He *had* brought reinforcements. Behind him were several other people from the nearby farms. Patty the fishmonger was there, of course. She had a nose for any kind of commotion.

And there were more. Bill must have raised the

291

alarm to the whole town. Etta appeared with her pa, the town baker. I'd bought bread from Etta at the market only days before, but it seemed a lifetime ago.

Fern and I stayed huddled beside the second trailer, keeping her hidden from view of the road. Although it was a relief to see familiar faces, I was nervous about how Fern would react. She was so big now that one misstep could cause a panic, and that was the last thing we needed.

Fern growled, a low rumble, as Charles, Mr Johnson and the squirrel-woman reappeared at the gates. Charles carried the cruel whip, the metal embedded knots clinking with each step. I pressed my hand against Fern's side, until she quietened.

To my surprise, Charles didn't appear at all fazed by the small crowd.

"Thank you all for coming along and for your concern," he said, in a clear, authoritative voice. "But everything here is under control. I have the situation in hand, at last."

He motioned for everyone to stand back, in such a commanding way that everyone immediately obeyed, making a space for him to walk through.

"No," I whispered. My voice had stuck in my

throat and at what a time. My skin prickled in fear, as his eyes slid over me and Fern.

"I have come to take these creatures away," Charles declared. His voice was different – loud, imposing. "As you have all realized, they are highly dangerous. I will be transporting them somewhere safe, where they can no longer terrorize your town." He gestured to Fern who had been hidden in the shadow of the trailer. "You can plainly see that these creatures are out of control."

The townspeople all turned and stared at Fern, at her towering size and enormous bulk.

"Is that ... the Direspire beast?" Patty gasped. She pressed her hand against her chest as if she was about to have a heart attack. "Good riddance, take them away, I say!"

There was a low murmur of agreement from the other people.

No! I wanted to shout. *You've got it all wrong!* I put one hand protectively around Fern's trunk.

"So, Lady Cavendish was keeping dangerous creatures all along," Bill said, mouth gaping as he took in the size of Fern. "It's about time she got rid of them!"

I had to find my voice. For Fern.

"He's stealing them!" I shouted, my heart racing.

Griff came and stood next to me. I could see the lump under his jumper, where Pinecone the pangolin was still hidden. He put his other arm around Fern, while jiggling on the spot.

Lady Cavendish seemed to shake out of her daze and strode up to the gathering throng. "Cora's right; this man is stealing from me. We intercepted the robbery so he locked us in the trailer. Those creatures are mine." Lady Cavendish swiped the splinters from her trousers and glared at Charles Linton. "I demand the return of them immediately."

"But the creatures *are* dangerous, isn't that so?" Patty said, eyeing Fern nervously. "Maybe it's the right thing, for this man to take them away."

More people from the surrounding farms were starting to arrive at the gates, on horseback and foot. The head teacher of my school strolled up the road with his terrier, who barked at the sight of Fern, straining at her leash. Everyone had similar expressions of awe and fear. They couldn't know that Fern wasn't the monster she seemed. I wanted everyone to love her, not be afraid of her.

"Fern isn't dangerous!" I said, my voice wobbling,

as everyone turned to stare at me. "But she's frightened. You have to give her some space!"

The baker, Etta's pa, shook his head. "And we're supposed to take your word for it? Look at the thing, it's huge! It could crush a person under one foot!" He shook his head. "I'm glad it's chained up, that's all I can say." Out of the corner of my eye, I spotted Tilly with her pack of friends. She stooped and picked something up from the ground.

She weighed it up in her hands and took aim, staring right ahead at Fern.

Before I could react, the rock whizzed through the air, hitting the pangea with a crack on her forehead where the daisies grew. The rock sliced through the daisies, leaving a gash of broken flowers.

With a fearsome roar, so loud I could feel it in my bones, Fern swung backwards, careening into the trailer behind her. There was an ear-splitting sound of splintering wood. I grabbed hold of Griff, pulling him back, away from the broken trailer.

The crowd went silent, as everyone stared at the ruins of the trailer.

"Where is Tempest?" I gasped. Hadn't Mr Johnson put the cage in that wagon? I leaped forward, but Lady Cavendish grabbed hold of me, wrapped her arm around my shoulders so I couldn't run towards the wreckage. I struggled against her, desperate to find Tempest. The trailer was a mess of twisted steel and splintered wood.

A flash of blue and I spotted him. The seacat crawled out of the wreck, where he stood wobbling on the grass, panting heavily. He was alive.

But then, to my surprise, Tempest took a running leap and clambered up on to Fern's back. The blue and black cat disappeared, hiding himself among the long grass and swaying ferns.

Lady Cavendish released her grip on my shoulders. She reached out to Bea who looped her arm in hers. "Thank goodness no one was hurt," Lady Cavendish croaked. Her face was paper white.

My relief at seeing Tempest escape unhurt was short-lived. From the broken trailer, came a scuffling sound. There was something else still in there.

The feeling of dread deepened. From the shattered wood and twisted metal, there came giant, spider-like legs, which probed the air.

Then, frighteningly quick, the fossil-feeder skittered out into the open. It was larger than I'd ever imagined, with a squat cockroach body the size of a bull, and eight crab-like legs. It was the colour of cave rock, and smelled like a burning bog fire, of rotten eggs and mud.

The creature dived forward. I couldn't move. I could only gawp, as the fossil-feeder charged on all eight legs, its jaws wide.

But it never reached me, or anyone else.

Fern, her hackles raised, broke free of her chains and thundered forward, bellowing at the fossil-feeder. She planted herself in the way, giving the crowd enough time to scatter.

Fern. She was protecting us. She roared at the fossil-feeder, stomping her feet, so that the ground trembled. The fossil-feeder scuttled backwards, its wispy feelers quivering.

Could she keep the creature at bay? I hoped she could, at least for long enough to get everyone away to safety. At that moment, I saw Pa and Ma riding up the road on Merlin, Ma clinging tight to Pa with a look of fierce determination.

"Pa, don't come any closer!" I shouted. Dogs barked, while horses bucked, sending their riders flying, and out of the corner of my eye, I spotted Mr Johnson and the squirrel-woman scarper, escaping down the road to Brambury Town. There was no time to chase them down, because while all attention was diverted, Charles had stepped into the fray.

I saw him raise his arm up, with his ringmaster's whip in hand. With a hiss, Charles's whip fizzed through the air. It slashed across Fern's face, and she bellowed.

Without missing a beat, Charles raised his whip again and it hissed in an arc through the air.

It caught the tree that stood proudly on Fern's back, wrapping around it like a black snake.

No! I rushed to Charles's side and grabbed hold of his arm, but he knocked me back effortlessly with a blow to the side of my face. Sharp pain bloomed, and I tasted blood.

"I *will* get the beast under control." Charles gritted his teeth and wrenched the whip, pulling it taut, his knuckles white with the effort.

There was a creak and a groan that could have come from Fern or me, then an almighty *crack*. The tree on Fern's back came away from the roots with a tearing, wrenching sound.

Fern toppled to her knees, with a keening cry that made my stomach roll. She was hurt, badly.

The tree lay next to her, its roots like broken bones. On her back, the space where the tree had grown trickled with blood as thick as molasses.

The scream sounded far away, but it was coming from me. I ran to her, throwing my arms around her neck. She groaned. I could smell the metallic blood and torn earth.

"That's enough." Charles grabbed the back of my shirt and dragged me back. "Get out of my way, girl, or you will be next." His face was contorted into a snarl. He raised the whip above my head.

I braced for the lash that would surely slice my skin open, but it never came.

I opened my eyes, to see that Fern had grasped hold of the whip with her trunk. Her trunk bloomed with blood where the metal-embedded knots had torn into her grey skin.

A bear-like roar sounded and Pa came charging through the crowd, a fearsome look on his face. Charles's face whitened and he moved like a shot, ducking into the crowd.

"Are you all right, Cora?" Ma grabbed hold of my chin, her hand trembling. She inspected my face. "You're bleeding!"

But it wasn't me who needed care, it was Fern.

I pressed my face against her mossy side. I could hear her heartbeat, fast and loud. She shuddered, and a shower of torn leaves rained down.

Then I stiffened, as someone shrieked behind me. "The creature, it's taken a child!"

In the commotion, I'd forgotten all about the fossil-feeder.

Chapter 32

The Fossil-Feeder

Patty cried out, "The creature, it's taken Tilly!"

Tilly. She always had to be the centre of attention. *Of course* it would be Tilly who got snatched by the fossil-feeder.

I scrambled to my feet and ran forward. The fossil-feeder had Tilly in its crab-like pinchers. Her body swung limply, like a ragdoll, and for a moment I feared the worst, but then I remembered; she was sedated by its venom. The fossil-feeder raised its cockroach head and snuffled at the air, jaws clacking. Then the fossil-feeder took off at a startling speed, towards Direspire Hall.

I cast my mind back frantically to *Creatures of the Four Realms* and realized that I knew where the fossil-feeder was headed. It was going home, back to the Deep Earth, where it had come from. And there was only one way to get there.

Lady Cavendish had told me the old covered well led directly to the Deep Earth. If the creature made it to the well, we'd never see Tilly again.

"Griff," I said. "Stay with Fern. Make sure she knows you're here, and that she's not alone."

Griff nodded, his face pale with fright. He took over my spot, wrapping his arm around Fern's trunk, his other arm still tucked around the lump of pangolin under his jumper.

Merlin had been tethered to the open Direspire gates. I ran to him and, using the gate as a boost, I jumped on to his back. I heard Pa call out, but I ignored him. There was no time to waste.

"Come on, Merlin, we need to go as fast as you've ever gone before!" I pushed the old horse into a gallop: past the fountain, towards the gated garden, where the whistling trees were.

Through the shrubbery ahead, I caught a glimpse of grey spider-legs and a whiff of rotten eggs. My heart quickened.

Next to Direspire Hall, I dismounted, leaving Merlin where he was safely away from any danger. Then, I followed the fossil-feeder, as it scurried past the shattered remains of the glasshouse.

It snuffled the air, tendrils trembling, as it made its way down the path towards the covered well, where Griff and I had collected seawater for Tempest's Pond only days before.

Fighting back my fear, I inched closer.

The well was in reach. I could see the wooden cover, mossy and riddled with woodworm.

The fossil-feeder scurried across the rotting wood panels, which creaked and groaned under its weight. It deposited Tilly, who slumped in a heap. Then, the creature began to gnaw at the wood with its jaws.

Carefully, I took a step on to the wooden boards. Then another. The wood shuddered under my feet. The smell of damp and rot from the creature was overpowering. I had to reach Tilly, before the fossil-feeder managed to gnaw through the wood. She was almost within grasping distance.

The creature was utterly focused on its task, busy trying to get back to the Deep Earth, where it belonged. I couldn't blame it. It had been used as entertainment in a travelling circus for years, and now it had a chance to go back home.

I nearly had Tilly within my grasp when a board

crumbled under my knee and I fell on to my hands and knees. The pieces of broken wood disappeared into the black hole of the well. I could feel the emptiness below me, the never-ending yawn.

"Not another step," came a familiar voice. Charles Linton. "I'll be damned if I let that creature escape."

Sweat beaded on my forehead. Shuffling forward on my knees, I grasped Tilly's feet with both hands and yanked her away from the fossil-feeder, who barely registered the loss of its prey, so intent was it on gnawing through the rotten wood. I shoved Tilly across the rotten slats, and over the lip of the well with every last ounce of my strength, where she tumbled to the safety of the ground.

Through the air came a whip lash. It spun out and caught on the fossil-feeder's legs.

The fossil-feeder trembled. Now that the wood was crumbling away, it could smell the Deep Earth. The boards were about to give way. Desperately, I lunged for the lip of the well, where I'd shoved Tilly to safety seconds before.

Too late. With a crack, the boards gave way underneath me.

And then I dropped downwards, hurtling

head-first towards the bottom of the black pit of the well, down to the Deep Earth.

To my relief and confusion, I jerked to a halt, and my whole body slammed into the wall, knocking the air from my lungs. I hung upside down, and could only watch as the fossil-feeder plummeted past, Charles Linton plunging down with it, still holding on to the whip. Even in the face of death, he refused to give up his creature. I kept my eyes on the pair of them, until they blinked out of sight, engulfed by the bottomless pit.

The fossil-feeder was finally going home.

"Cora!" Griff appeared above me. "You're safe!"

I twisted around, the blood rushing to my head, and found myself staring up at Fern, who had her trunk wrapped around my leg.

"Fern!" I gasped. "I thought I was done for." My head spun, black spots dancing before my eyes.

Then, slowly, she hauled me up, towards the circle of light, where hands grasped hold of me and pulled me to safety.

I was on solid ground again. Ma and Pa were there. They hugged me, the three of us wrapped together. Too many voices talked at once. Some of the farmers helped block up the well, with fallen branches from the whistling trees, while others crowded around Tilly, who was blearily opening her eyes, coming around from the creature's sedation.

I pulled away from Ma and Pa and ran to Fern's side, where she'd curled up on the ground. I collapsed next to her and spread my arms around her, as far as they would reach. Her eye was swollen shut. Her plants were broken and there were wounds and gashes on her flanks. She sighed as I pressed my wet face against hers.

"You saved me, Fern. You saved me and Lady Cavendish and Griff and Bea and all of those people." A ragged breath surged up my throat. I couldn't lose her. "Please, you have to be all right."

Gently, Fern curled her trunk around me and closed her other eye.

It hurt to breathe. Through my tears, I swept my palm across Fern's cheek, brushing the broken vines away from the deep slashes on her face.

For once, Echo the macaw was quiet. From the long grass on Fern's back, emerald eyes peered down at me. Tempest.

I talked to Fern in a language all of our own, promising her that I would make sure that she was never going to be confined again, that I would make sure that she was free, as long as she didn't give up, not now.

I felt her move. She took a deep breath in and opened her eye, the one that wasn't swollen closed. In the brown depth, there was a new energy.

My heart skipped. *You're going to be all right*, I whispered. I stood up and, shakily at first and then with renewed strength, Fern heaved to her feet beside me.

Chapter 33
Setting Free

It wasn't long before everyone in the town knew the story of the traitorous butler, the thieving circus master and the beast of Direspire that saved a creature keeper from the well.

The gates of Direspire Hall remained open, and, without Mr Johnson spreading fearful rumours of bloodthirsty creatures, Lady Cavendish managed to acquire the services of an excellent gardener, and a small army of housekeepers to help begin the formidable task of sorting through the clutter of Direspire Hall, which Bea was elated about.

Soon, the chaos of the Hall started to take shape, as the curtains were mended and windows flung open, candlesticks polished and piles of clutter gradually reduced. Lady Cavendish and

Bea still bickered about what to discard and what to keep, and Direspire Hall still remained a trove of strange and wonderful things, but you could see past the piles of books, at least. Even the pale faces of Lady Cavendish's ma and pa seemed to look more cheerful, as they were gradually joined by portraits of the pangolin, Tempest, the moonbirds, and, suspended in the air, a glass dragon in flight. To my delight, Griff was promoted to second-in-command creature keeper. After everything we had been through, I knew that I couldn't do the creature keeping job without him. His confidence around the creatures grew with every day. We made a great team.

The money that I made as creature keeper was enough to fix the cottage thatch and to keep Bella and the herd warm and fed. I would never have to worry about Bella being sold ever again. Only one thing remained for me to do, a promise that I'd made.

Fern waded out into the sea. On her back, Tempest sprawled, sunning himself after his morning swim.

Although she had lost the sight in one eye, the rest of Fern's wounds had healed. And by now she had grown to the size of a tiny islet. Lady Cavendish's parents had been right all along.

She floated on the water, gently bobbing on the waves.

Griff and I stood on the pebbled beach, watching Fern. Overhead the gulls swirled in the currents, where I caught a glimmer every now and then. Brittle, the glass dragon, had also taken residence on Fern's back, along with Tempest and Echo. The plants were growing back, and a tiny sapling had sprouted in the hollow of the torn-out tree.

Nearby, Lady Cavendish had set up her easel, where she could paint Fern on a large canvas, with green and blue sweeps of her paintbrush, her nose scrunched in concentration.

Watching Fern swimming in the gentle waves, I knew it was the right time.

"We need to set them free," I said to Lady Cavendish. "Fern and Tempest, the moonbirds, and the rest of the creatures belong in the wild."

"Fern wouldn't last in the wild, she's vulnerable," Lady Cavendish muttered, dotting daisies on to the canvas in bright spots of yellow. "She's safe here."

I shook my head. The wild needed her as much as she needed the wild.

"Your parents' book said that the pangea can become home for all sorts of extraordinary plants and creatures, like Tempest and Echo and Brittle. She needs to be free."

"And how will she survive the journey back to The Sea Realm?" Lady Cavendish dunked her paintbrush in the glass water jar and swirled it around. "She's likely to encounter all sorts of dangers along the way. There are plenty of creature collectors out at sea, with harpoon ships, capable of capturing a living island."

"Maybe Fern just needs a little help," I said, the idea only just occurring to me. "Maybe she could use a few creature keepers to guide her."

Lady Cavendish looked down at me sharply. "Are you suggesting we undo all the work that my parents did, and take the creatures back to the four realms?"

I grinned back at her. I nodded.

Lady Cavendish narrowed her black-as-a-crows-eyes at me. "Very well. If you're up for the task, I think we should begin planning our trip."

I cupped my hands around my mouth and called out to Fern.

Herrrooooooooooooooooooaaaaahhhhhooooo

Fern raised her trunk, spouting seawater high into the air.

Herrrooooooooooooooooooaaaaahhhhhooooo

From Fern's back, Echo took flight, soaring into the air with Brittle the glass dragon. I smiled to myself. It was time to take them all home.

Acknowledgements

I have so many people to thank who helped bring *The Creature Keeper* to life, especially as I never imagined I'd be writing the story during a global pandemic.

Thank you to my editors; Lauren Fortune, Jenny Glencross and Genevieve Herr for all your hard-work, vision and your brilliance. I feel so incredibly lucky to be able to work with you all.

Thank you to the brilliant Scholastic team: Bleddyn Sion for another cracking cover design, Pete Matthews for your eagle-eyed proofread and Harriet Dunlea for your fantastic PR work. Flavia

Sorrentino, thank you so much for creating the utterly gorgeous cover artwork.

Thank you to all the hard-working booksellers, teachers and bloggers who supported me through my debut year, and a huge thank you to Scott Evans, Lily Fae, Louise Nettleton, Samantha Thomas and Em Steers at Tink's Reviews who have all been incredibly kind and encouraging.

Thank you to my superstar agent Alice Sutherland-Hawes for everything you do.

Thank you to the swaggers, whose support, wit and mindboggling talent has become my writing fuel through the tough days. Long may the gifs, goats and silliness reign.

Thank you to my parents, whose resilience, creativity and humour never ceases to amaze me.

To my siblings, Josh, Bethany, Hannah and Jordan. I'm so proud of each of you.

To my partner Josh, for understanding me so well, and Jack and Daisy, my wild and happy beasts.

And thank you, Readers. You are all extraordinary creatures.

Damaris Young studied on the
writing for young people MA at Bath
Spa University, where she wrote
her debut novel *The Switching Hour*,
whose fictional setting was inspired
by the landscape and legends of
Southern Africa, where she spent her
childhood. She now lives in Bristol
with her partner and two dogs.

Find her on Twitter: @damarisyoung